Vertue Rewarded

Vertue Rewarded ;

OR, THE

IRISH Princeſs.

A NEW

NOVEL.

She ne're ſaw Courts, yet Courts could have undone
with untaught Looks, and an unpractiſ'd Heart ;
Her Nets, the moſt prepar'd, could never ſhun,
For Nature ſpread them in the ſcorn of Art.

Gond. lib. 2. Cant. 7.

LONDON,

Printed for *R. Bentley,* at the
Poſt-houſe in *Ruſſel-ſtreet,*
in *Covent-Garden.* 1693.

VERTUE REWARDED;
OR,
THE IRISH PRINCESS

[Anon]

edited with an introduction and notes by

Ian Campbell Ross and Anne Markey

FOUR COURTS PRESS

Set in 10.5 pt on 13 pt Bembo for
FOUR COURTS PRESS LTD
7 Malpas Street, Dublin 8, Ireland
www.fourcourtspress.ie
and in North America for
FOUR COURTS PRESS
c/o ISBS, 920 N.E. 58th Avenue, Suite 300, Portland, OR 97213.

A catalogue record for this title
is available from the British Library.

ISBN 978–1–84682–213–1 hbk
978–1–84682–215–5 pbk

Printed in England
by Antony Rowe Ltd, Chippenham, Wilts.

Contents

The Literature of Early Modern Ireland series

Titles in the series:
Faithful Teate, *Ter Tria*, ed. Angelina Lynch (2007)
Henry Burkhead, *Cola's Furie*, ed. Angelina Lynch and Patricia Coughlan (2009)
Richard Nugent, *Cynthia*, ed. Angelina Lynch and Anne Fogarty (2010)
William Dunkin, *The Parson's Revels*, ed. Catherine Skeen (2010)

Early Irish Fiction, *c.*1680–1820

Also published in the series:
Sarah Butler, *Irish Tales* (1716), ed. Ian Campbell Ross, Aileen Douglas, &
   Anne Markey

Forthcoming titles in the series:
Thomas Amory, *The Life of John Buncle, Esq.* (1756), ed. Moyra Haslett
Henry Brooke, *Juliet Grenville; or, the history of the human heart* (1774), ed.
   Sandro Jung

Preface

Irish prose fiction of the long eighteenth century has only recently begun to receive the attention it merits. While such names as Swift, Goldsmith and Edgeworth have long been familiar to readers of Irish (and British) literature, many other writers – born, educated, or living in Ireland – produced a substantial and imaginatively varied body of fiction from the late-seventeenth to the early-nineteenth century. This series aims more fully to indicate the diversity and breadth of Irish literature in the period 1680–1820 by providing critical editions of a range of exemplary works of prose fiction. In so doing, it will indicate the role the early novel played in inventing Ireland for readers at home and abroad, while offering new perspectives on the literature and history of these islands.

Each title in the series will contain a carefully-edited text, together with a critical introduction, a select bibliography, and comprehensive notes, designed for scholars and students of Irish writing in English, of the English novel, and all those concerned with Ireland *c*.1680–*c*.1820.

Aileen Douglas
Moyra Haslett
Ian Campbell Ross
January 2010

Acknowledgments

The editors gratefully acknowledge the award by the Irish Research Council for the Humanities and Social Sciences of a Small Research Grant (2008–10) for Early Irish Fiction, c.1680–c.1820. We also gratefully acknowledge financial assistance from the Long Room Hub, Trinity College Dublin, and the Centre for Irish-Scottish and Comparative Studies, Trinity College Dublin.

For their generosity in answering queries, the editors are grateful to Sonia Anderson, John Brannigan, Andrew Carpenter, Aileen Douglas, Moyra Haslett, Leanda de Lisle, Giles Mandelbrote, Hugh Mayo, William Molesworth, Proinsias Ó Drisceoil and Liam Ó Duibhir.

The frontispiece illustration of the title-page of the first edition of *Vertue Rewarded; or, the Irish Princess* (1693) is reproduced by permission of the British Library.

Introduction

One of the earliest examples of Irish prose fiction, *Vertue Rewarded; or, The Irish Princess* (1693) anticipates many of those features that would make the new literary form of the novel so appealing to eighteenth-century readers. A fiction that develops around a romance plot in which a young Irish woman finds her virtue 'rewarded' by marriage to a foreign prince, after he finally renounces his attempt to seduce her, may not sound exceptional. That the work, which appeared in London as part of a 12-volume collection of 'modern novels' published by the bookseller Richard Bentley, is set in a carefully documented Ireland at the time of the Williamite wars more easily commands readers' attention. Still more intriguing is the fact that both the principal narrative and the interpolated story of Cluaneesha take place in the town of Clonmel; the settings being the summer of 1690 and an unspecified moment in Gaelic Ireland's pre-Norman past respectively. And that a much longer interpolated narrative, 'The Story of Faniaca', draws extensively and titillatingly on the Inca Garcilaso de la Vega's celebrated account of Inca history, recently translated into English as *Royal Commentaries* (1688) by a former Chief Secretary for Ireland, the diplomat and scholar Sir Paul Rycaut, confirms *Vertue Rewarded* to be a work exceptional for its time, and perhaps any other. Mediating highly charged contemporary events by way of well-established literary conventions, fusing ancient stories with recognizably modern locations, and coupling geographical settings both local and exotic, *Vertue Rewarded* challenges its readers with a narrative at once distinctive, and distinctively new.

Irish prose fiction can nevertheless be dated back several decades before *Vertue Rewarded*: at least to the six volumes of *Parthenissa* (1654–65), an heroic romance by the soldier and politician, Roger Boyle (1617/18–1687), first earl of Orrery. Orrery's best-known fiction followed such fashionable and often still more voluminous French models – *L'Astrée* (1607–28) by Honoré d'Urfé (1567–1627), *Cassandre* (1642–5) and *Cléopâtre* (1647–58) by Gautier de Costes, sieur de La Calprenède (c.1609–63), and *Le Grand Cyrus* (1649–53) and *Clélie* (1654–60) by Madeleine de Scudéry (1607–1701) – that celebrated the valour and amours of their high-born characters in appropriately elevated language. For *Parthenissa*, whose first part was printed in Waterford in 1651 (an edition now lost) as for his uncompleted *English Adventures* (1676), Roger Boyle adopted the pseudonym 'A person of honour'.[1] The same pen-name was used by his younger brother, Robert Boyle (1627–91), whose fame as a scientist and philosopher far exceeds his renown as an author of fiction. Written several decades before it appeared in print in 1687, *The Martyrdom of Theodora, and of Didymus* was nonetheless a work greatly esteemed in the late-seventeenth and eighteenth centuries.[2] Boyle's was a carefully considered attempt at a true Christian history: a work that endeavoured to avoid the extravagances of prose romance, while engaging the attentions of the reader in an edifying, Christian story by a judicious use of history, elaborated in the manner of contemporary fiction.[3] Based on the story of a fourth-century martyr first told in St Ambrose's *De virginibus* (377) and more recently retold in John Foxe's *Acts and Monuments* (1563; 9th ed. 1684), better known as 'The Book of Martyrs', Boyle's reworking of the story was much admired. It appeared not only in a second edition in 1703 but in the 1744 complete edition of Boyle's works, with the result that the Revd Thomas Morell used it as the basis of the fine libretto he wrote for what George Frederick Handel would make one of his greatest English oratorios, *Theodora* (1750).[4]

The heroic romance remained so much in fashion throughout the seventeenth century that the second edition of *The Æthiopian History* (1686), by the third-century Greek writer Heliodorus, appeared under the title *The Triumphs of Love and Constancy: A Romance containing the Heroick Amours of Theagenes & Chariclea* (1687). It was Nahum Tate (c.1652–1715), the Trinity College Dublin-educated poet and playwright, who became Poet Laureate in 1692, who translated into English the last five of the ten books of this work. That the taste of readers of fiction was changing, however, is indicated by the work of a younger contemporary of Tate.

In the year before *Vertue Rewarded* was published, William Congreve (1670–1729), born in England but educated at Kilkenny School and Trinity College Dublin, published a prose fiction *Incognita: or, Love and Duty Reconcil'd* (1692). The work is better known today, perhaps, for its preface than for the fiction itself. That preface, however, has a singular importance in Congreve's attempt at an early critical distinction between the novel and the romance: two terms that would, for decades to come, be often interchangeable, or subsumed under a more general description of contemporary prose fiction as the 'new species of

---

1 See Rolf Loeber and Magda Loeber with Anne Mullin Burnham, *A Guide to Irish Fiction 1650–1900* (Dublin: Four Courts, 2006), pp 171–2: Deana Rankin, *Between Spenser and Swift: English Writing in Seventeenth-Century Ireland* (Cambridge: Cambridge University Press, 2005), p. 151.

2 [Robert Boyle], *The History of Theodora, and of Didymus. By a Person of Honour* (London, 1687).

3 For Boyle's elaborate justification of his work, see 'Such an Account of the following Book, sent with it to a Friend, as may serve instead of a Preface', *The History of Theodora*, pp [iii]–[xxviii].

4 Robert Boyle, *Love and Religion Demonstrated in the Martyrdom of Theodora, and of Didymus. The Second Edition Corrected* (London, 1703); *The Works of the Honourable Robert Boyle*, 5 vols (London, 1744).

writing'.⁵ It is a distinction immediately applicable to *Vertue Rewarded*. 'Romances', writes Congreve, 'are generally composed of the Constant Loves and invincible Courages of Hero's, Heroins, Kings and Queens, Mortals of the first Rank, and so forth; where lofty Language, miraculous Contingencies and impossible Performances, elevate and surprize the Reader into a giddy Delight'. By contrast, novels 'are of a more familiar nature; Come near us, and represent to us Intrigues in practice, delight us with Accidents and odd Events, but not such as are wholly unusual or unpresidented, such which not being so distant from our Belief bring also the pleasure nearer us'.⁶ With its Florentine setting, and characters named Aurelian, Hippolito, Incognita and Leonora, however, *Incognita* more readily invites comparison with romance than with the novel its title page proclaims it to be.

The case of *Vertue Rewarded* is different. The title, it is true, would seem to link the work with contemporary heroic romance, with the Irish princess joining a list of high-born protagonists of Bentley's 'modern novels', whose titles include *Queen of Majorca*, *Queen of Polonia*, *Queen Blanch of Spain*, *Homais Queen of Tunis*, and *Princess of Fez*. Despite its title, however, *Vertue Rewarded* offers a principal narrative of a 'more familiar' nature – alongside others decidedly exotic – surprising readers by its firm grounding of romance elements in settings that are by no means nominal but clearly identified, rather, in time and space. Taking pains from the outset to depict a contemporary social framework – the arrival of the Williamite forces, the billeting of the officers in the town, the entertainments offered them by a grateful citizenry – the work contains its romance elements within the conventions of more modern fiction. Located so precisely, and unexpectedly, in Clonmel, in a period that extends from the end of July to the end of August 1690, *Vertue Rewarded* shows a concern with exactly those elements of formal realism that were for long held virtually to define the novel but which, though occasionally present in earlier writing, are more immediately discernible in the fiction of later decades, most notably in the work of Daniel Defoe in the 1720s. In its Irish provincial setting – *all* provincial settings for fiction remained suspect to some readers throughout the eighteenth century – and its concentrated time-span of barely a month, *Vertue Rewarded* has no rival among contemporary or most eighteenth-century works of prose fiction.

While the novel is notable both for the nature of its historical content and for the speed with which it rendered political events in fictional form, *Vertue Rewarded* could nevertheless draw on a range of even more speedily published eyewitness accounts of the summer of 1690. Those months had seen the decisive events in the wars in Ireland between the Roman Catholic forces of the

---

5 See, for example, Henry Fielding, *The History of the Adventures of Joseph Andrews*, 2 vols (London, 1742), I, pp vi , xvii. Fielding does not use the phrase in its complete form but it was familiar to readers within a decade; see *An Essay on the New Species of Writing founded by Mr. Fielding* (London, 1751).

6 William Congreve, 'The Preface to the Reader', *Incognita* (London, 1692), pp viii, viii–ix.

deposed James II and the Protestant army of the Dutch prince, William of Orange, who had ascended the English throne along with James's Protestant daughter, Mary. It was on 1 July 1690 (Old Style) that William III won a famous victory at the Battle of the Boyne, causing the defeated Jacobites to abandon the north and east of the island and regroup west of the river Shannon, taking the heavily-fortified city of Limerick as their stronghold. Though William quickly mounted a siege of the city, in the hope of capturing it swiftly, the combination of strong Jacobite resistance and bad weather led him to lift the siege at the end of August, renewing his assault only in 1691, when Limerick finally capitulated.

Accounts of these momentous events in the histories of Ireland and Great Britain soon found their way into print. They included an anonymous *Account of the Victory Obtained by the King in Ireland* (1690), Samuel Mullenaux's *A Journal of Three Months Royal Campaigns of His Majesty in Ireland together with a True and Perfect Diary of the Siege of Lymerick* (1691), and *A True and impartial History of the most material Occurrences in the Kingdom of Ireland during the last two years with the Present State of both Armies: published to prevent mistakes, and to give the World a Prospect of the future success of Their Majesties Arms in that Nation; written by an eye-witness to the most remarkable passages* (1691). This last work would prove perhaps the most enduring and influential eyewitness account of the Williamite wars in Ireland. Originally published anonymously, it was extended by a history of the events of 1691, in *A continuation of the impartial history of the wars of Ireland from the time that Duke Schomberg landed with an army in that Kingdom, to the 23d of March 1691/2, when Their Majesties proclamation was published, declaring the war to be ended … together with some remarks upon the present state of that kingdom*, published in London in 1693. Both this, and a consolidated, work, *An impartial history of the wars in Ireland, with a continuation thereof* (1693), reveal the author to have been the Revd George Story, chaplain to Sir Thomas Gower's (later the earl of Drogheda's) regiment. It is a work that confirms – and was most likely the source of – much information about the war in Ireland in 1690 found in *Vertue Rewarded*.

That a great quantity of printers' ink would be expended on accounts of the 1688–91 military campaigns was to be expected, even if the fact that a writer of fiction should so quickly draw on these accounts was not. In its accomplished interweaving of romance and history, however, *Vertue Rewarded* might be thought to epitomize the literary ideals described in the preface to another of Bentley's 'modern novels', *The Perplex'd Prince*. There, the author writes that 'in the acquiring of Knowledge, nothing can be more helpful than Reading, and among other sorts of Books wherein the diligent Reader greedily searches and inquires after Knowledge, *Novels*, Romances, and Allegorical Writings are not the least useful … Some … are curiously designed to point out the Nature of Vertue and Vice, with the Benefits of the one and the Mischiefs of the other'.[7]

---

7 [Anon.], *The Perplex'd Prince* (?1682), in *Modern Novels*, 12 vols (London, 1692–3), II, 'To the Reader', pp [vii]–[viii].

The narrative of *Vertue Rewarded* begins with the entry of part of the Williamite army into Clonmel in late July 1690. The commander of the force is the Prince of S——g described as one 'the smallness of whose Principality not affording him an Income agreeable to his High Title, and Higher Mind … resolved to acquire that Plenty which his Fortune had denied him, and show by his Valour, that he was nothing beholding to her for giving him Titles' (p. 40). At the head of his men, he rides along the main street of the town and sees, watching him from a window, a beautiful young woman, who 'alone drew the admiration of all the Men, as she did the envy of the Women' (p. 45), whose name, he will later discover, is Marinda. Like that of other characters in *Vertue Rewarded* – Celadon or Astolfo, for instance – the name Marinda is drawn from the realm of pastoral romance narrative, making the contrast between it and the Prince of S——g all the more striking to contemporary readers. If the thoughts of most of those readers might first have turned to the great Frederick Herman, first duke of Schomberg, the 'ablest soldier of his age',[8] who had been commander-in-chief of William III's army in Ireland, those more politically aware would quickly have recalled that Marshal Schomberg had been killed at the Battle of the Boyne on 1 July.[9] Some few readers might also have been more particularly intrigued, for the commander of the Williamite troops that entered Clonmel at the end of July 1690 was Count Meinhard Schomberg (1641–1719), third son of the first duke.[10] The *roman à clef* or 'secret history' was a popular enough form in the late-seventeenth and early-eighteenth centuries: Madame de Lafayette's *La Princesse de Clèves* (1678) is perhaps the most celebrated example, while among English-language works, Delarivier Manley's *The Secret History of Zarah* (1705) would offer a thinly-concealed narrative concerning relations between Sarah Churchill, the ambitious wife of the Duke of Marlborough, and Queen Anne.[11] In the case of *Vertue Rewarded*, however, the use of the name S——g for the prince who falls in love with Marinda, but believes her too far beneath him in social rank to marry, seems to have been rather an authorial tease than anything more revealing. Certainly, it is impossible to match the personal life of Count Meinhard Schomberg with that of the Prince of S——g or,

8 Daniel Defoe, *The True-born Englishman: a Satyr* (1701), l. 1011.
9 The death of the duke of Schomberg at the Boyne is eventually mentioned in *Vertue Rewarded*, but only close to the end of the novel; see p. 129.
10 Meinhard Schomberg would be created baron of Tara, earl of Bangor, and duke of Leinster in 1691, before becoming third duke of Schomberg in 1693.
11 Manley was also author of *Secret Memoirs and Manners of Several Persons of Quality, of Both Sexes from the New Atalantis, an Island in the Mediterranean* (1709), while both Jane Barker and Eliza Haywood also wrote 'secret histories'. For differently-focused accounts of the 'secret history', see also Dale Spender, *Mothers of the Novel* (London and New York: Pandora, 1986), esp. pp 47–111; Jane Spencer, *The Rise of the Woman Novelist* (Oxford: Basil Blackwell, 1986), pp 41–74; Michael McKeon, *The Origins of the English Novel, 1600–1740* (Baltimore and London: Johns Hopkins University Press, 1987), pp 54–5, 61; and Margaret Anne Doody, *The True Story of the Novel* (London: HarperCollins, 1997), p. 30.

indeed, that of another high-ranking officer of the Williamite army, known in the novel as *K—k*, with that of Major-General Percy Kirk, the officer who commanded the land forces at the siege of Derry.[12]

The early introduction of the name *S——g* nevertheless alerts readers of *Vertue Rewarded* to the novel's military and historical dimensions, which will form a significant part of the fiction. Drawing on one or more of the near-contemporary accounts of the military campaign in Ireland in 1690 to ensure accuracy, *Vertue Rewarded* anticipates later developments in English-language prose fiction, inviting comparison with, say, Defoe's *Memoirs of a Cavalier; or, A Military History of the Wars in Germany and the Wars in England, from 1632 to 1648* (1720), a proto-historical novel for which Defoe quarried materials from Bulstrode Whitelocke's *Memorials of the English Affairs* (1682), along with *The Memoirs of Edmund Ludlow* (1698–99) and the Earl of Clarendon's *History of the Rebellion* (1702–4).[13]

No more than *Memoirs of a Cavalier*, however, does *Vertue Rewarded* simply offer realistic reportage in fictional guise. Nor does the depiction of the Prince of *S——g* draw wholly on romance conventions. Instead, we find throughout a consummate blend of romance and history. So while awaiting further orders, the Prince of *S——g* will remain in Clonmel, giving the opportunity for the attempted seduction plot to develop. When his orders arrive, he will start for Limerick at the head of his men to take part in the first siege of that city, allowing both for the renewed protestations of love and varied and accurate summaries of the actual military campaign in Ireland – including a positively inflected account of Patrick Sarsfield's raid on the English wagon train at Ballyneety that emphasizes the Irish commander's bravery and daring – contained in the ensuing epistolary correspondence between himself and Marinda. When the siege is lifted, his return allows for an opportunity – when confronting rapparees, or Catholic irregulars, who were indeed active in the area surrounding Clonmel[14] – of saving Marinda's life. If the romance plot continues to engage readers of contemporary prose fiction, however, the accretion of his-

---

12 The novel does, however, raise the question of *K—k*'s 'constancy' in love in what could conceivably be a reference to Percy Kirk's well-known inconstancy in political allegiance, manifested in his desertion of James II for William of Orange; see p. 151 below, n. to '*K—k*'.

13 See Arthur W. Secord, 'The Origins of Defoe's *Memoirs of a Cavalier*', in Secord, *Robert Drury's Journal and Other Studies* (Urbana, IL: University of Illinois Press, 1961), pp 72–133.

14 See [George Story], *A true and impartial history of ... the Kingdom of Ireland during the last two years* (London, 1691) p. 137, and James Shirley, *The true impartial history and wars of the Kingdom of Ireland its situation, division into provinces; shires &c., its ancient inhabitants, manners, customs and the state it was in at its being first invaded and conquer'd by the English in the reign of K. Henry II: with the several revolts and rebellions of the natives and by what means they have been reduced to obedience in the reign of our several kings and queens: but most particularly relating to all the memorable skirmishes, battels, sieges ... since the grand revolution under the reign of Their Present Majesties K. William and Q. Mary* (London, 1692), pp 124–8, for instance.

torical detail anchors this plot in a recognizable version of contemporary life. In a striking passage, the author writes: 'I trust, the Reader will not think it prejudicial to our Prince's Honour, to come back without taking the Town, this was not his fault, but his Fortunes; the days of Errantry are past, nor have our Warriours now, such Swords as those Knights of old, that could hew a way through the thickest walls, and do wonders greater than our Age will believe: Our Prince did not pretend to impossible Exploits' (p. 114), so recalling Congreve's contemporary distinction between romance and the novel.

It was explicitly as a 'novel' that *Vertue Rewarded* appeared in 1693. Then it took its place in the twelfth and final volume of the series *Modern Novels* (1692–3), published in London by Richard Bentley, whom John Dunton dubbed 'Novel Bentley'.[15] Since the near-fifty novels that make up the twelve volumes were mostly reprints of earlier romance-like texts – often translations, mainly from French – it could be argued that *Vertue Rewarded* is in fact the most 'modern' of all the novels in the series, and not simply because it was demonstrably a late addition, and the only work to bear the date 1693 on its separate title-page.[16]

The plot of *Vertue Rewarded* is nonetheless one familiar from both earlier and later fiction. The book's very title, indeed, has reminded readers of a far more famous novel whose subtitle this is: Samuel Richardson's *Pamela; or, Virtue Rewarded* (1740). Richardson's hugely popular account of the resistance of the young servant girl, Pamela, to the attempts by her master Mr B. to seduce her, which reaches its climax when Pamela is rewarded for her virtue by marriage, does indeed recall the earlier work. (Whether it was actually influenced by it, as has been suggested, is more doubtful, and it might equally well be noticed that both plots echo that of Cinderella, a story whose most celebrated version, Charles Perrault's 'Cendrillon', would appear in the same decade as *Vertue Rewarded*.)[17] If here the would-be seducer is a prince, rather than a private gen-

---

15 For Bentley, see Giles Mandelbrote, 'Richard Bentley's copies: the ownership of copyrights in the late 17th century', in Arnold Hunt, Giles Mandelbrote & Alison Shell, *The Book Trade & its Customers, 1450–1900: Historical Essays for Robin Myers* (Winchester: St Paul's Bibliographies, 1997), pp 55–94, and Marja Smolenaars, 'Richard Bentley', in *Oxford Dictionary of National Biography* (Oxford: Oxford University Press, 2004).

16 Examination of the copy held in the British Library (12410.c.29) shows that the work it replaced was not a 'novel' at all but rather a political work whose title – given as *Means to Free Europe from French Slavery* – allows for its identification as the anonymous *Means to Free Europe from the French Usurpation; and the Advantages which the Union of the Christian Princes has Produced, to Preserve it from the Power of an Anti-Christian Prince* (London: Printed for Richard Bently [sic], 1689).

17 For possible connections between *Vertue Rewarded* and Richardson's novel, see Paul Salzman, '*Vertue Rewarded* and *Pamela*', *N&Q*, New Series, 26 (1979), 554–5; Salzman, *English Prose Fiction, 1558–1700* (Oxford: Oxford and New York, 1985), p. 340; Hubert McDermott, 'Introduction' to McDermott (ed.), *Vertue Rewarded; or, the Irish Princess*. Princess Grace Library: 7 (Gerrards Cross: Colin Smythe, 1992), esp, pp xxviii–xl; and Thomas Keymer and

tleman, and the virtuous young girl a gentlewoman rather than a servant, the discrepancy between their social positions is nevertheless emphasized through-out as the barrier that keeps them apart – and the plot going – for the duration of the novel. While Marinda zealously guards her virtue, the prince must resolve the conflict he perceives between love and his worldly interest before subordi-nating his 'high title' to his 'higher mind', offering at last the only terms the young Irishwoman will accept: those of marriage.

What the novel offers in addition to this romance plot, however, is not only its uniquely specific contemporary setting but a series of interpolated tales, of which two stand out. Both are female narratives and both are characterized, initially, by a seemingly oblique relationship to the story of Marinda.[18] The tale of Cluaneesha (pp 62–4) and 'The Story of Faniaca' (pp 72–96) also share chronologically or geographically remote settings: pre-Norman Ireland and sixteenth-century Peru, respectively. While disparate in other respects, these two interpolated tales not only share an emphasis on female virtue – a familiar enough trope in romance – but also use their carefully specified settings to reflect on the contemporary understandings of the cultural poles of civilization and barbarism.

The story of Cluaneesha, set in Clonmel, tells of a princess, daughter of a king of Munster, wrongly accused of fornication whose virtue is miraculously proved by her drinking from a local well. Telling this tale, while the lovelorn Prince of S——g is resting near the spring, the narrator concludes by affirming that the well was 'long after reverenced … for the quality it had of discovering Unchastity', though as after-times became increasingly wicked, 'by disuse this Well lost its Fame, and perhaps its Vertue' (pp 63, 64). The narrator then undertakes to 'no longer tell such tales' and returns his attention to the Prince, who overhears Miranda simultaneously confess her love for him and protest her own virtue.

At first glance, the tale of Cluaneesha seems a digression from the main nar-rative. To those familiar with the conventions of story-telling in Irish, it might also appear a piece of genuine *seanchas*, or local lore, that confirms the author's familiarity not only with Clonmel and its environs, but with Gaelic culture more generally.[19] First impressions can be deceptive. While the particular well described in *Vertue Rewarded* has a plausible basis in fact, the legend of Cluaneesha turns out to be an authorial fiction for which no source exists. Contrary to the narrator's assertion, in fact, the story does not feature in any of the chronicles of Irish history to which the author could have had access at the

Peter Sabor, *Pamela in the Marketplace: Literary Controversy and Print Culture in Eighteenth-Century Britain and Ireland* (Cambridge: Cambridge University Press, 2007), esp. pp 177, 183–4. See also Charles Perrault, *Contes de ma mere l'oye* (Paris, 1697).

18 Besides the two main interpolated tales, there are also the maid's tale (pp 52–6) and the tale of Astolfo (pp 126–30).

19 See J.H. Delargy, 'The Gaelic Story-Teller', *Proceedings of the British Academy*, xxxi (1945), pp 6–7. For the use of *seanchas* in an eighteenth-century Irish novel, see Ian Campbell Ross, 'Thomas Amory, *John Buncle*, and the origins of Irish fiction', *Éire-Ireland*, 18:3 (1983), 71–85.

time the novel was written, even in the Irish language.[20] That the tale is authorial invention can be inferred most directly from the fact that the central character in the supposed legend bears a name that might *seem* Irish but is, in fact,
impossible. A name that does not exist outside of the pages of *Vertue Rewarded*,
'Cluaneesha' would at most be not a personal but a place name – though to
confuse matters still further the name *could* be directly related to the well or
spring that features in the story, deriving from 'cluain' (a clearing in a wood) and
'uisce' (water).[21] Despite the narrator's insistence on the veracity of the tale and
its source in Irish legend, the story of Cluaneesha in truth draws on no authentic Irish material whatsoever. If the tale of the Irish princess convinced its first
English readers, who had little with which to compare it, and might still deceive
modern non-Irish speaking readers, its source – if it has or indeed needs one –
is not folklore but fakelore.[22]

If the tale is *not* Irish, why does this matter? The answer lies in the fact that
the story of Cluaneesha serves to reflect both on Ireland's past and on the present moment. First, the story promotes a positive view of the civility of ancient
Irish society that is possibly unique in English-language fiction of the late-seventeenth century. The conclusion of the story makes the point decisively.
Though Cluaneesha renounces her intention of entering a nunnery in favour of
ascending her father's throne, the author insists that 'the Well was long after reverenced, and for the quality it had of discovering Unchastity, it was much
resorted to, adding by way of explanation that:

> other Nations report'em) were too nice in Amour to take a polluted
> Wife to their Bed (pp 63–4).

The versions of pre- and even post-Norman Gaelic Ireland against which the
tale of Cluaneesha is to be measured are, it is clear, hostile English accounts of
the country, by such writers as Edmund Spenser, Edmund Campion, or
Meredith Hanmer – though charges that women were common property or
chastity of no consequence were made of many, if not all, 'barbarous' societies.[23]

---

20 The story does not appear in major Irish language annals, such as *Lebor Gabála Érenn*, *Annála
Rioghachta Éireann* or Seathrún Céitinn's *Foras Feasa ar Éirinn*, all of which, in any case, were
available only in manuscript form at the end of the seventeenth century.

21 We owe this suggestion to Dr Proinsias Ó Drisceoil. 'Cluaneesha' might also derive from
Cluain Meala, the 'plain of honey', the Irish name of Clonmel itself. Siobhán Kilfeather,
meanwhile, suggested a derivation from the Irish for Íte's Meadow, 'Sexuality, 1685–2001',
Field Day Anthology of Irish Writing, ed. Seamus Deane et al., 5 vols (Derry: Field Day, 1991
and Cork: Cork University Press, 2002), 4, p. 767.

22 'Fakelore' is a term coined to describe a synthetic product claiming to be authentic oral tradition but actually tailored for mass edification; see Richard M. Dorson, *Folklore and Fakelore*
(Cambridge, MA. and London: Harvard University Press, 1976), p. 5.

23 Campion alleged of the Irish that, even following the introduction of Christianity, 'the
'Honourable state of marriage they much abused'; *The Chronicle of Ireland* in *The Historie of*

The partiality of English accounts of Ireland was a common complaint in the late-seventeeth century, despite Irish counter chronicles such as Peter Walsh's *Prospect of the State of Ireland, from the Year of the World 1756 to the Year of Christ 1652* (1682) and Roderic O'Flaherty's *Ogygia* (1685).[24] Just over two decades later, the Irish novelist Sarah Butler would make a similar point still more vigorously in another fiction set in pre-Norman Ireland. In *Irish Tales* (1716), Butler defends her presentation of her Gaelic Irish characters by noting that:

> altho' they may [not] seem so now, in the Circumstances they lie under, (having born the heavy Yoke of Bondage for so many Years, and have been Cow'd down in their Spirits) yet ... once *Ireland* was esteem'd one of the Principal Nations in *Europe*.[25]

In contrast to the author of *Vertue Rewarded*, however, Sarah Butler certainly did have access to positive accounts of Gaelic Ireland, for the novel is based on a detailed and ingenious reworking of material from the *Foras Feasa ar Éirinn* by the seventeenth-century writer Seathrún Céitinn (Geoffrey Keating), which the author knew in one of the manuscript versions circulating – in Irish or in English – before the work finally achieved publication, in an English translation by Dermod O'Connor (possibly with the assistance of John Toland), in 1723.[26] Sarah Butler looked to manuscript sources to substantiate her view of the Gaelic Irish as polite. Remarkably, the less well-informed author of *Vertue Rewarded* was so anxious to present a positive view of the native Irish as 'nice' – here, civilized in their attitudes towards female chastity and marriage, in contrast to barbarous societies – that in the absence, or inaccessibility, of genuine material to support this thesis, a legend was simply invented, attributed vaguely to 'an ancient *Irish* chronicle', and tricked out to appear authentic.

Equally pointed is the setting of Cluaneesha's story, which prompts the telling of the tale. Early in the novel, we read that the Prince – already in love with Marinda but uncertain as to how to behave towards someone who is a gentlewoman yet his social inferior – leaves Clonmel in search of solitude:

Ireland, collected by three learned authors viz. Meredith Hanmer Doctor in Divinitie: Edmund Campion sometime Fellow of St Johns College in Oxford: and Edmund Spenser Esq (Dublin, 1633), p. 16.

24 Peter Walsh, *A Prospect of the State of Ireland, from the Year of the World 1756 to the Year of Christ 1652* (London, 1682), and Roderic O'Flaherty, *Ogygia, seu Rerum Hibernicarum chronologia ...* (London, 1685).

25 Sarah Butler, *Irish Tales*, ed. Ian Campbell Ross, Aileen Douglas and Anne Markey (Dublin: Four Courts Press, 2010), p. 39; see also 'Introduction', esp. pp 18–20.

26 Geoffrey Keating [Seathrún Céitinn], *The General History of Ireland*, trans. Dermod O'Connor (London, 1723); see also Diarmaid Ó Catháin, 'Dermot O'Connor, Translator of Keating', *Eighteenth-Century Ireland/Iris an dá chultúr*, 2 (1987), 67–87.

when he had walked about half a mile, he found himself on top of a Hill, whence after having looked a while on the adjacent Town, and with a curious Eye searched out that part of it, which his admired Beauty made happy with her presence, he laid him down under the shade of two or three large Trees, whose spreading Boughs nature had woven so close together ... they seemed to have been the first planted there, for the shelter of those who came thither to drink; for just by there bubbled up a clear and plentiful Spring ... (pp 61–2).[27]

This well has more problematic significance than might be immediately apparent to novel readers today. Importantly, it links the central narrative of the prince and the future princess Marinda (which takes place in 1690) and the interpolated story of the earlier Irish princess Cluaneesha (set at an unspecified moment in the pre-Norman past). Venerated as a source of healing, holy wells had a very real, if sometimes contested, importance in Irish life, being particularly associated with mass demonstrations of popular Roman Catholic devotion. *Vertue Rewarded* was published just two years before the passing of the first of the Penal Laws, or the Laws in Ireland for the Suppression of Popery, designed to secure the religious, social, economic and political ascendancy of the Protestant – specifically Anglican – community in Ireland. As part of the extension of the penal legislation, a law would be passed in 1705 to the effect that 'whereas the superstitions of popery are greatly increased by the pretended sanctity of ... wells to which pilgrimages are made by vast numbers, all such meetings and assemblies shall be adjudged riots, and unlawful assemblies, and punishable as such'.[28] Far from being merely an element of local colour, in other words, the holy well is an ideologically charged intrusion into the romance narrative that contains it, its principal interest lying in the cultural and political implications of the interpolated tale associated with it.

Less than two years after the 1691 Treaty of Limerick confirmed the power of the Anglo-Irish in Ireland, the story of Cluaneesha introduces an earlier Irish princess, to whom Marinda will eventually become a modern counterpart, whose story revolves around the moral centre of the novel – virtue and its rewards – while engaging with the theme of political legitimacy. In so doing, Cluaneesha's story anticipates the critical examination of the relationship between colonizer and colonized that characterizes the much longer, interpolated narrative in *Vertue Rewarded*: 'The Story of Faniaca'.

27 The perceived significance of the episode is confirmed by its inclusion in Kilfeather, 'Sexuality 1685–2001', 4, pp 767–8.

28 2 Ann c. 6 (1703), sec. 26. See also, for example, Michael P.Carroll, *Holy Wells and Popular Catholic Devotion* (Baltimore, MD, and London: Johns Hopkins University Press, 1999), Elizabeth Healy, *In Search of Ireland's Holy Wells* (Dublin: Wolfhound, 2001), and Diarmuid Ó Giolláin, 'Revisiting the Holy Well', *Éire-Ireland*, 40:1 & 2 (2005), 11–41.

Related by the eponymous South American Indian woman, 'The Story of Faniaca' begins in the Amazonian region of Antisuyu in the sixteenth century, at the time of the Spanish conquests. Faniaca tells how she was brought up in an area bordering on the Inca empire, saved the life of a Spanish officer, with whom she at last fell in love, and how she accompanied him on his escape from execution, to the coast, where she was captured, and taken to Spain, eventually making her way, in search of her lover, via England to Clonmel.[29] If the provincial Irish setting of *Vertue Rewarded* was unfamiliar to a London audience – settings of other of the 'modern novels' published by Richard Bentley in his compilation included Portugal, Hungary, Spain, Majorca, Poland, Hungary, Tunis and Fez – the area of what is now Peru would certainly have appeared exotic to an English novel readership, despite the South American setting recently used by Aphra Behn in her *Oroonoko; or, The Royal Slave* (1688). If *Oroonoko* – with its mix of romance narrative and recent colonial history is now known to draw partly on Behn's personal experience of Surinam,[30] then 'The Story of Faniaca' is also firmly based on 'true' history: in this case the recently-published *Royal Commentaries* of the Inca Garcilaso de la Vega (1539–1616), in the translation by Sir Paul Rycaut.

The Royal Commentaries of Peru (1688) is Sir Paul Rycaut's consolidated translation of Garcilaso's *Comentarios reales de las Incas* (Lisbon, 1609) and *Historia General del Peru* (Cordoba, 1617). The choice of source is doubly intriguing, both for the narrative of *Comentarios reales* and for the identity of its translator, a former Chief Secretary for Ireland. Most significantly *Royal Commentaries* offers a decidedly critical view of Spanish colonialism in south America while recognizing the Incas as imperialists in their turn. So, the clash of cultures described by Garcilaso is not only that between the Incas and the colonizing Spanish but between the empire of the Incas and that of other American Indians, here specifically the inhabitants of Antisuyu, in the upper Amazon. Garcilaso was the son of a Spanish conquistador, Sebastián Garcilaso de la Vega, and an American Indian mother, Isabel Suárez Chimpo Ocllu. An Inca princess, Isabel was related to both of the two last Inca rulers, the Inca Huáscar and Atahuallpa. Sebastián Garcilaso de la Vega later married off the mother of his eldest son to a com-

---

29 Faniaca's tale involves a considerable telescoping of its source material, which involves not just a single lifetime but runs from pre-Inca society, through the heyday of the Inca empire, its overthrow by the Spanish, and takes the action up to the late-seventeenth century; for Sarah Butler's comparable telescoping of history in the interests of fictional narrative, see *Irish Tales*, pp 25–7.

30 The charge that Behn never set foot in Surinam was made by Ernest Bernbaum in 'Mrs Behn's Biography, a Fiction', *PMLA* 28 (1913), 432–53. Subsequent refutations and clarifications include: J.A. Ramsaran, '"Oroonoko": A Study of the Factual Elements', *Notes & Queries* 1960, 7 (4), 142–5; Bernard Dhuicq, 'Further Evidence on Aphra Behn's Stay in Surinam', *Notes & Queries*, 1979, 26 (6), 524–6; and Dhuicq, 'New Evidence on Aphra Behn's Stay in Surinam', *Notes & Queries*, 1995, 42 (1), 40–1.

moner, to facilitate his own marriage to a Spanish woman. In these biographical details are contained the seeds of the stories of both Marinda, the heroine of *Virtue Rewarded*, who marries the Prince of S——g, once he has abandoned his attempts to seduce her, and of Faniaca, who marries her Spanish lover.[31]

The story of Cluaneesha, we have seen, only *appears* to be derived from a genuine Irish chronicle. By contrast, the tale of Faniaca – understood by modern readers as no more than extravagant fiction[32] – draws closely for its historical setting on Rycaut's *Royal Commentaries*. The pagan daughter of an American Indian priest in the province of Antis, Faniaca falls in love with a Spanish conquistador, Astolfo, who has made common cause with the Incas in their attempt to conquer the people of Antisuyu. Saving the life of Faniaca's father by shooting dead one of his own Inca soldiers, Astolfo gains the gratitude of the priest, and the love of Faniaca. Permitted to leave Antisuyu, Astolfo later returns, only to be captured and condemned to death. Faniaca pleads for his life but when Astolfo's return is taken as evidence of an incorrigible desire to impose his will on her people, she can find no way to save him but to effect his escape and her own. Fleeing to the coast, the lovers are captured by buccaneers and, despite Faniaca's pleading, separated.

While the tale of Faniaca and her lover has no basis in known fact, the account of Antisuyan society has clearly demonstrable origins in *Royal Commentaries*. In *Virtue Rewarded*, we read:

> My Name is *Faniaca*, my Father was a *Brachman*, an *Indian* Priest in the Province of *Antis*, which Countrey having never been conquered by the *Incas*, kept up the ancient Barbarity, not being Civilized by their Laws, as those Nations were, who had yielded to their Government. (p. 73)

That the Antisuyans had never been conquered by the Incas is made clear in *Royal Commentaries*, where Garcilaso sums up his account of Antisuyan barbarity by explaining: 'Such are the Idols and manner of living of these Brutes, because the Government of the *Incas* was never received into their Countrey,

---

31   See Inca Garcilaso de la Vega, translated by Paul Rycaut, *The Royal Commentaries of Peru, in two parts the first part treating of the original of their Incas or kings, of their idolatry, of their laws and government both in peace and war, of the reigns and conquests of the Incas, with many other particulars relating to their empire and policies before such time as the Spaniards invaded their countries: the second part, describing the manner by which that new world was conquered by the Spaniards ... written originally in Spanish by the Inca Garcilasso de la Vega; and rendered into English by Sir Paul Rycaut, Kt* (London, 1688), 'The Translator to the Reader', p. [iii].

32   The story of Faniaca has been described as 'a lurid interpolated tale of Peruvian cannibalism [that] looks forward if anything to Swift', see Thomas Keymer and Peter Sabor, p. 183. For a differently focussed account of Swift and Peruvian cannibalism, see Ian Campbell Ross, '"A very knowing American": the Inca Garcilaso de la Vega and Swift's *A Modest Proposal*', *Modern Language Quarterly*, 68:4 (2007), 493–516.

nor hath it any Power there at this day'.[33] The author of *Vertue Rewarded* simi-
larly draws directly on *Royal Commentaries* when Faniaca continues her account
by informing her listeners that whereas the Incas worshipped the sun, the Antis
were a polytheistic people with several deities, 'the two chief of which were the
Tyger, and a large Serpent, which we called *Amaru*' (p. 74), closely following
Garcilaso's 'In those Provinces of *Antis* they commonly worshipped Tygers for
their Gods, and great Serpents, much thicker than a Man's Thigh, and twenty
five, or thirty foot in length … called *Amaru*'.[34]

To such varied pieces of political explanation or exotic local colour, Faniaca
adds a much more chilling account of the practices of her people. '[I]t was our
custom', she relates, 'to sacrifice Human Blood; they commonly fed on nothing
else but Captives, and if we had no Captives, we were forced to find them the
same sort of Blood from among our selves' (p. 74). As Faniaca herself reveals,
however, the Antisuyans lived in a state of near-continual war – not just with
the Incas but also with the Spanish and their Indian allies who 'sent Parties far
into our Countrey to take Booties, and make discoveries of the Land, in order
to a farther Conquest' (p. 74) – so that prisoners are rarely in short supply.

The present war is nonetheless one the Antisuyans are losing as Faniaca's
story opens, with the Spanish from their 'great Colony' at 'Cosco' [i.e. Cuzco]
encroaching so far into Antisuyu that 'they had driven us over the *Madalena*, that
great River, being very deep, of a strong swift Current, and at that place about
a League broad' (p. 74).[35] During an attack, Astolfo is captured and sentenced to
death in precisely the manner so vividly described in *Royal Commentaries*. As the
work is little known today and virtually every detail has its counterpart in *Vertue
Rewarded*, the passage is worth citing at length:

> those who live in *Antis* eat Mens Flesh, and are more brutish than the
> Beasts themselves, for they know neither God, nor Law, nor Vertue …
> When they take any in the War, if he be an ordinary Fellow, they quar-
> ter him, and divide him to be eaten by their Wives, Children and
> Servants, or perhaps sell him to the Shambles; but if he be of Quality or
> Noble, they call their Wives and Children together, and like Officers of
> the Devil, they strip him of his garments, and tye him to a stake, and then
> alive as he is, they cut him with Knives, and sharp Stones, paring off slices
> from the more fleshy parts, as from the Buttocks, Calves of the Legs, and
> the brawny places of the Arme; then with the Bloud they sprinkle the
> principal men and Women, and the remainder they drink, and eat the
> Flesh as fast as they can, before it is half broiled, lest the miserable Wretch

33 *Royal Commentaries*, Book I, chap. iv, p. 7.
34 *Royal Commentaries*, Book IV, chap. xvii, p. 119; see also below, note to p. 74 '*Tiger … Serpent
    … Amaru*'.
35 Cf. *Royal Commentaries*, Book VIII, chap. xxii, p. 338.

should dye before he hath seen his flesh devoured, and intombed in their bowels: The Women, more cruel and inhumane than the Men, wet the nipples of their Breasts with the bloud, that so the Infants which suck them may take a share of the Sacrifice. All this is performed by way of a religious Offering with mirth and triumph, till the Man expires, and then they complete the Feast in devouring all the remainder of his Flesh and Bowels, eating it with silence and reverence, as sacred, and partaking of a Deity. If in execution of all this torment the Patient was observed to sigh and groan, or make any distorted faces, they broak his Bones, and with contempt threw them into the fields and waters; but if he appeared stout, and enduring the anguish and pains without shrinking at them, then his Bones and Sinews were dryed in the Sun, and lodged on the tops of the highest Hills, where they were deified, and Sacrifices offered to them.[36]

This, we may need to remind ourselves, is 'history'. No wonder then that when Denis Vairasse d'Allais, author of the imaginary travels, *L'Histoire des Sévérambes* (1675–7), insisted on the close relationship between factual and fictional histories, he had his publisher declare that 'the Histories of *Peru*, *Mexico*, *China*, &c. were at first taken for Romances by many, but time has shewed since that they are verities not to be doubted of'.[37] Since Astolfo has seemingly returned as an enemy, however, Faniaca initially declares not only that he should suffer death but tells him that 'to shew how little I pity you, I will go to see you Sacrificed, and eat the first bit of you my self' (p. 79). Only after realizing that Astolfo's return was prompted by gratitude and his love for her does Faniaca undergo a change of heart. Faced with witnessing the death of her lover in barbaric circumstances, she substitutes another of the Spanish prisoners, who is then put to death:

> the poor wretch was cut to pieces slice after slice, and lived long enough to see his own Flesh broiled, and eaten by the Company; you must think this was a terrible sight to the rest, who saw by their Companion what they were to suffer. (pp 82–3)

Faniaca's father has perceived his daughter's ploy, however, and marks out Astolfo as the next victim. A fire is lit to cook his flesh, he is tied to a tree, and the priest takes a knife to his captive, drawing blood, at which point Faniaca faints, putting a temporary end to the proceedings. The following day, Faniaca distracts the guards with 'a large Pot full of pleasant Liquor, made of our Sacred Plant the *Coca*' (p. 84)[38] and, with the help of two servants, enables her lover to escape, while she joins him in his flight.

36 *Royal Commentaries*, Book I, chap. iv, p. 7.
37 Quoted by McKeon, *The Origins of the English Novel*, p. 111.
38 Cf: *Royal Commentaries*, Book IV, chap. xvii, p. 119.

Much of the background to this and the ensuing narrative, which involves an encounter with buccaneers, continues to have a discernible basis in the *Royal Commentaries*. Yet when Faniaca is forcibly separated from Astolfo, the narrative model changes decisively once more, this time to folktale.[39] In Spain, the sea captain presents Faniaca to his wife as a servant. During his subsequent absence, Faniaca relates how she has learned the art of telling the future from her father.[40] She tells her mistress, who scoffs at Faniaca's supposed powers, that her husband will return home the following day. Later that evening, Faniaca witnesses the wife entertaining a young lover to a hearty supper when, to their consternation, the captain returns home. The lover is hidden in a chest and to allay her husband's suspicions, the wife claims to have prepared supper in preparation for his homecoming, which had been predicted by her maid, Faniaca. The soothed cuckold then orders that the chest, which he believes to contain sea biscuit, be brought to his ship. Faniaca averts potential disaster for her mistress by claiming that the chest now contains an evil spirit that she had inadvertently raised during her fortune-telling. As a result of this deception, the lover escapes, and the adulterous wife avoids detection. The virtuous Faniaca is now free to negotiate her passage to England in pursuit of her own lover, Astolfo, whom she will eventually marry.

Ultimately, Faniaca's story demonstrates that virtue – here, fidelity in love – is the most powerful weapon available to a powerless woman. Once again, what initially appears to be a digressive narrative serves to underscore the main theme of the novel. And, like the story of Cluaneesha, it does so in the context of a complex engagement with shifting notions of colonized and colonizer, barbarism and civilization.

In its interweaving of romance narrative, Irish and Peruvian history, fakelore and folklore, *Vertue Rewarded* supports Michael McKeon's argument that seventeenth-century fiction characteristically draws on a range of generic categories, including history and romance.[41] The self-consciousness with which the author deploys his materials is indicated in his 'Preface to the Ill-natur'd Reader', where he declares that:

> the main Story is true, I heard of a Gentleman who was acquainted with the *Irish* Princess, and knew all the Intrigue, and having from him so faithful a Relation of it, I made the Scene the very same where it was

39 The story of Faniaca, the sea-captain, his wife, and her lover echoes the international group of folktales – a trickster surprises an adulteress and her lover – found in many cultures, ages, and languages, classified under the Aarne/Thompson system as Type 1358; see Stith Thompson, *The Types of the Folktale: A Classification and Bibliography* (Helsinki: Suomalainen Tiedeakatemia, Academia Scientiarum Fennica, 1964), p. 403. For a more detailed account of the folk elements in this part of Faniaca's story, see below, nn. to p. 90, '*I saw her sitting at table*' and p. 92, '*enter into it himself*'.

40 For the role of women as fortune-tellers, see *Royal Commentaries*, Book I, chap. vi, p. 10.

41 See McKeon, *The Origins of the English Novel*, esp. pp 25–64.

transacted, the time the same, going on all the way with the *Truth*, as far as conveniency would permit; I only added some few Circumstances, and interlined it with two or three other Stories, for variety sake. (p. 37).

The author of *Vertue Rewarded*, in other words, is here at odds with the simple averral of truth that characterizes the opening paragraph of Aphra Behn's *Oroonoko*, where Behn writes:

> I do not pretend, in giving you the history of this royal slave, to entertain my reader with adventures of a feigned hero, whose life and fortunes fancy may manage at the poet's pleasure; nor in relating the truth, design to adorn it with any accidents, but such as arrived in earnest to him: And it shall come simply into the world, recommended by its own proper merits, and natural intrigues; there being enough of reality to support it, and to render it diverting, without the addition of invention.[42]

In *Vertue Rewarded*, we find a more open acknowledgement of the distinctive blend of materials that make up the novel. So, the story of Cluaneesha, in which the writer has invented material purportedly taken from an Irish chronicle, is nonetheless set within a modern narrative in realistic mode that demonstrably draws on local knowledge of Clonmel during the Williamite wars. 'The Tale of Faniaca', meanwhile, makes use of recently published and admired history, set off by further interpolations employing international folktale motifs. The clearly discernible morals of the two main interpolated narratives, however, serve to reinforce the theme of the central plot – the story of the Prince of S——g and Marinda – emphasizing the practical rewards of virtue, in stories that insistently cross national, cultural, and class boundaries.

However conventional it may at first appear, with its romance plot, *Vertue Rewarded* offers complex accounts of different human societies, riven by war, conquest, imperial ambition, and political and religious difference. The conclusion of the fiction, with its multiple marriages, therefore constitutes an imaginative attempt to heal such divisions, by means of the union of a European prince to a member of the Irish protestant gentry; of the English officer Celadon to Marinda's cousin Diana; and of the Spanish conquistador Astolfo to the American Indian Faniaca, the wedding celebrations being deferred, at Faniaca's request, until she has been baptized (the eventual marriage of the 'fair Convert' seemingly conducted by a Roman Catholic priest).

While *Vertue Rewarded* has been seen as simply endorsing the values of the Irish Protestant settler community, such a reading does little justice to the intricacies of the historical perspective in evidence throughout. [43] The account of the

---

42 Aphra Behn, *Oroonoko; or, The Royal Slave: a True History* in *Oroonoko and Other Writings*, ed. Paul Salzman (Oxford and New York: Oxford University Press, 2004), p. 6.

43 See Hubert McDermott, 'Introduction', p. xi; Nicholas Canny, 'Identity Formation in Ireland:

failure of the first siege of Limerick illustrates the point. With the 1690 campaigning season drawing to a close, Patrick Sarsfield left Limerick with a force of 600 horsemen to mount a surprise attack on the Williamite siege train, resulting in the destruction of two of the eight siege guns and the loss of the wagons, gunpowder and other supplies. Contemporary English accounts of this exploit varied but, at worst, Sarsfield's raid was condemned as little better than an atrocity. So in James Shirley's *True impartial history and wars of the Kingdom of Ireland* (1692), readers were told that Sarsfield, with a strong party, 'set upon ... the Convoy, [and] killed divers of the Waggoners, not sparing their Wives, with their Children in their Arms'.[44] The account offered by the author of *Vertue Rewarded* is very different. Writing to Marinda, the Prince declares that Limerick would soon be taken, since heavy cannon had been called for, and were on their way, while the English army awaited only a breach in the walls to storm the city. 'But', the narrator continues, 'Fortune had otherwise ordered it, for *Sarsfeild* with an unusual Bravery, marched with a small Body of Horse, farther into that part of the Country which was Subjected to the *English* Power, than they suspected he durst; surprized the Convoy, and cutting them to pieces, burnt them, their Carriages and Provisions, (which they brought for the Army) to ashes; some of the Carriages he nailed up, and burst the rest'. The result was that the army 'raised the Siege; his Majesty went for *England*; his Forces retired to their winter Quarters, and our Prince to his Mistress' (pp 113, 114).

If this is a very differently nuanced view of one of the best-known incidents in the war of 1688–91, then *Vertue Rewarded* offers caution for the peace also. When a fashionable young man comes down to Clonmel from the metropolis in search of a bride, the 'Breeding' he displays 'elevated him so far above' even his provincial counterparts, in his own eyes, 'that they did look like our wild *Irish* to him' (p. 54). By the 1690s, there was a long-established tradition of representing the native – Gaelic, Catholic – population as 'wild Irish', from the work of Gerald of Wales (Giraldus Cambrensis), through Spenser, Campion, Hanmer and many others.[45] The dangers of creating divisions not only within Ireland as a whole but even with the protestant community are deftly suggested here. More importantly, an awareness of the ease with which a 'civilizing' mission can turn into barbarism runs through the entire novel.

The point is most tellingly made by the story of Faniaca, with its double colonizing narrative: of Spaniards and Incas, and of Incas and the inhabitants of Antisuyu. Throughout *Royal Commentaries*, both the Inca Garcilaso and his translator Rycaut make the reader aware of a conflict between civilization and

the Emergence of the Anglo-Irish', Nicholas Canny and Anthony Pagden (eds), *Colonial Identity in the Atlantic World, 1500–1800* (Princeton: Princeton University Press, 1987), p. 202; Kilfeather, 4, p. 767; Keymer and Sabor, p. 183.

44 James Shirley, *The true impartial history ... of Ireland*, p. 87.

45 See Joep Th. Leerssen, *Mere Irish and Fíor-ghael: Studies in the Idea of Irish Nationality* (1986; Cork: Cork University Press in association with Field Day, 1996).

barbarism, seen from opposing perspectives. The Spaniards justify their actions by claiming to bring civilization to the Incas, while the Incas consider the earlier and concurrent expansion of their own empire as an attempt to civilize the population of Antisuyu (and other American Indian peoples). A laudatory account of Inca civilization had indeed been offered very recently by Sir William Temple, whose 'On Heroick Virtue' (1690) offered a positive reconsideration of four 'exotic' empires ranging from China to Peru.[46]

A close reading of Garcilaso's account in the original or in Rycaut's translation – Temple most likely drew mainly on the earlier abridgment in *Purchas his Pilgrimes* (1625)[47] – makes it hard to regard either of these civilizing narratives as tenable, at least in simple form. If the inhabitants of Antisuyu – like all pre-Inca peoples – are frequently characterized as barbaric, then the expansion of the Inca empire prefigures the Spanish conquest in its dependence on high levels of violence. By making Faniaca an inhabitant of Antisuyu, however – instead of an Inca, as might have seemed more familiar to the original audience, and easier to integrate into a short romance[48] – the author of *Vertue Rewarded* chooses a heroine from the most barbarous people in his historical source and yet shows her to be capable of sensibility, courage, gratitude, intelligence, fortitude, and fidelity.

In *Vertue Rewarded*, all ends well. Yet the multiple marriages with which *Vertue Rewarded* concludes are not driven solely by the demands of romance narrative. Rather, all three stories exemplify Margaret Anne Doody's contention that seventeenth-century fictions operate at the nexus of the public and the private, the author of *Vertue Rewarded* joining Madeleine de Scudéry or Aphra Behn as writers whom Doody understands as 'politically conscious and analytical', understanding life itself as a political affair.[49] The union of the English officer Celadon and the Irish gentlewoman Diana suggests the close ties that should bind Ireland to the metropolitan society (the author could not know how quickly these ties would loosen, as Swift would reveal in *The Story of the Injured*

---

46 The four non-Christian civilizations treated of by Temple were China, Scythia, Arabia, and Peru; for Peru, see *The Works of Sir William Temple, Bart.*, 2 vols (London, 1720), i, pp 205–11.

47 Samuel Purchas, *Hakluytus Posthumus; or, Purchas His Pilgrimes*, 20 vols (Glasgow: MacLehose and Sons, 1905), 17, pp 311–412.

48 Peru was the object of considerable interest in the seventeenth and eighteenth centuries. Jean Baudoin's translation of Garcilaso into French, *Le commentaire royal* (1633–50), was known in England to, among others, John Locke, who cited it in the second treatise of his *Two Treatises on Government* (1690). At a more popular level, John Dryden and Robert Howard had offered a fanciful account of war between the Incas and Aztecs in *The Indian Queen* (1664), a work later produced as a semi-opera, with music by Purcell, in 1695.

49 Doody, *The True Story of the Novel*, p. 263. See also Lennard J. Davis, *Factual Fictions: the Origins of the English Novel* (New York: Columbia University Press, 183); J. Paul Hunter, *Before Novels: the Cultural Contexts of Eighteenth Century English Fiction* (New York: W.W. Norton, 1990); and Rachel Carnell, *Partisan Politics, Narrative Realism, and the Rise of the British Novel* (Basingstoke: Palgrave Macmillan, 2006).

Lady (1707; pub. 1746) in which England, represented as a deceiving male lover, deserts the virtuous lady, Ireland, who is undone 'half by Force, half by Consent', for the ill-favoured, disloyal Scotland).[50] The marriage between the Prince of S——g and Marinda suggests the high estimate the settler community had of itself in the wake of the Williamite wars. In doing so, however, it not only brings the Irish narrative full circle but points up an ambiguity in the novel's title, offering readers a *second* princess, a successor to the virtuous Cluaneesha, who had ruled in Ireland in the distant past. That the Prince of S——g is a European ruler whose principality will not support him in the manner he desires ensures that he will settle in Ireland, confirming the contemporary perception of Ireland as a country whose very identity is to be understood in terms of a dynamic of repeated conquest.[51] It also reminds the settler community that its future has been secured by another Protestant, European prince, William of Orange, husband of Mary, daughter of the Roman Catholic James II.

The most striking of the three nuptials with which *Vertue Rewarded* concludes, however, is that between Astolfo and Faniaca. There can, surely, be no other work of fiction in English where one of the principal female figures, eventually set up as a paragon of virtue, has earlier threatened, with complete seriousness, to eat the man she eventually marries. As an inhabitant of Antisuyu, Faniaca belonged to the most barbarous of barbarous societies, despised as much by the Incas, as by the Spanish, one of whom she will marry. Since the Middle Ages, it had been a source of complaint that English settlers intermarried with the native Irish and, instead of civilizing them, became *hiberniores hibernis ipsis* or more Irish than the Irish themselves. As one Munster planter had complained earlier in the seventeenth century, settlers 'by marriage with the Irish ... became mere Irish again'.[52] Faniaca's tale wholly reverses the trajectory of this narrative of moral and cultural decline. Following the transference of her allegiance from her own barbarous people to the civilizing Spanish, her mastery of their language, and of English, her natural virtue, and her conversion to Christianity, Faniaca acts as a guarantee that marriage can be a means of raising once more a formerly polite, later barbarous, people to a state of civility.

That *Vertue Rewarded*, set in Ireland and published in London, should have melded folklore and fakelore with abundant local detail, drawn in part from a carefully documented account of the Williamite wars in Ireland in the summer of 1690, and a notable critique of European colonial history told from the viewpoint of the conquered, translated (partly in Ireland)[53] by a former Chief

---

50 Jonathan Swift, 'The Story of the Injured Lady' in *The Prose Works of Jonathan Swift*, ed. Herbert Davis et al. (Oxford: Basil Blackwell, 1939–68) vol. 9, *Irish Tracts 1720–23 and Sermons* (1948), pp 1–9 (5).

51 See *Vertue Rewarded*, p. 40; Canny, 'Identity Formation', p. 159.

52 Quoted in Canny, 'Identity Formation', p. 179.

53 In a letter written from Dublin Castle, Rycaut noted that he was pressing on with his translation of Garcilaso 'so often as I find the least leisure'; see Rycaut to Christopher Wilkinson, 18

Secretary for Ireland, is remarkable enough. That it should have used the romance form as the basis for a cautionary tale of colonial overreaching, interrogating the attempted distinction between civilization and barbarism that underpinned contemporary European im perial expansion in Ireland, as elsewhere, makes *Vertue Rewarded* still more extraordinary. The need in the 1690s for just such a cautionary tale, directed at an English or Protestant settler community so shortly to embark on the implementation of harsh penal legislation designed to contain the 'wild Irish' – a people yet not so 'barbarous ... as the partial Chronicles of other Nations report 'em' – cannot be doubted. For modern readers, resituating this London-published, English-language work in Irish and south American colonial contexts reveals *Vertue Rewarded* to be among the first and most imaginative works of Irish fiction.

May 1686, BL, Lansdowne MS 1153 A, f 33, cited by María Antonia Garcés, 'The Translator Translated: Inca Garcilaso and English Imperial Expansion', in Carmine G. di Biase (ed), *Travel and Translation in the Early Modern Period* (Amsterdam: Rodopi, 2006), p. 216.

A note on the text

The text of the present edition follows, as closely as possible, that of the first edition of *Vertue Rewarded*, using the British Library copy (12410.c.29) included in Volume XII of the 12-volume set, *Modern Novels*, published in London by Richard Bentley. The volumes bear the publication dates 1692–3, each title having an individual and separately dated title page, but only *Vertue Rewarded* bears the date 1693. The British Library copy was compared with the copy held by the Bodleian Library (8° S 178(2)).

A small number of emendations have been made to copy-text and are listed on p. 155. The only exceptions are as follows:

a) the first edition of *Vertue Rewarded* was published in 12mo and was unparagraphed, breaks in the text occurring only with the setting of verse, letters, and the interpolated tale, 'The Story of Faniaca'. An unparagraphed text would have made the present edition so densely printed as to be almost unreadable, so that paragraphing has been introduced, though this has been kept to a minimum, to preserve as much as possible of the textual continuity of the original.

b) the conventions indicating direct speech in the 1693 edition are extremely erratic, as is the case with much seventeenth-century printing: at times, quotation marks run down the left-hand margin of the text in the manner familiar in seventeenth and eighteenth-century printing; at others, direct speech is indicated by italicization; elsewhere, direct speech is not marked off in any way from the surrounding text. Here, an editorial decision has been made simply to indicate the beginning and end of passages of direct speech, using quotation marks, leaving interpolated locutions – '(said I)', '*replyed the Lady*', and so on – as they appear in the text. Other than the correction of obvious errors, noted in the List of Emendations, there has been no regularization of spelling or punctuation – though where obsolete spellings might cause modern readers difficulty the more normal modern spelling is given in the notes.

Vertue Rewarded;

OR, THE

IRISH Princess.

A NEW

NOVEL.

She ne're saw Courts, yet Courts could have undone
with untaught Looks, and an unpractis'd Heart;
Her Nets, the most prepar'd, could never shun,
For Nature spread them in the scorn of Art.
Gond. lib. 2. Cant. 7.

LONDON,
Printed for *R. Bentley,* at the
Post–house in *Russel-street,*
in *Covent-Garden.* 1693.

THE

Dedicatory Epistle

TO the Incomparable

*MARINDA.**

Madam,

THIS Novel throws it self at your Feet, and pays you Homage as its Master's Representative: It has been the product of some leisure hours, and will I hope do me this second kindness, to divert you in the Reading, as it did me in the Making. I need not, as others, give any reason for the Dedication; since to be made by me, is sufficient to entitle it yours: But that is not the only claim it can lay to your Favour; for in describing the *Marinda* of this Novel, I borrow from you, not only her Name, but some of the chief Beauties I adorn her with: Though you may imagine she had no mean ones of her own, since (being but a private Gentlewoman) she could by their help alone make so sudden a Conquest over the Heart of a Prince, who had certainly (in so many Courts as he had been in) seen very agreeable Faces, set off with the additional Splendor of Quality, yet none of them had that effect over him, which hers gained without those advantages. Besides, her true Character suits very well with you: She was an Innocent Country Virgin,* ignorant of the Intrigues and Tricks of the Court Ladies; her Vertue, like yours, untainted and undecayed, needed none of their Artificial Embellishments to guild it over; and that Innocence which appears eminently in both of you, as little wants these Ladies Artifices to set it off, as you do their *Fucus** for your Faces; since true Innocence is as far beyond Dissimulation, as your Colour is beyond all the Paint of the Town; in both of these you give Nature as signal a Triumph over Art, as ever she had in any two things whatsoever. I wish I could liken you to her in one thing more; that is, That your

Servant were of as high Quality as hers; but this wish is made
meerly for your sake: For to me, as you are more precious than
a Crown, so is the Title of a Prince inferiour to that Glorious
one, of being the

Humblest of your Servants.

The PREFACE

TO THE

Ill–Natur'd READER.

THE Dutchess of Suffolk* *entertaining once at her Table the Bloody* Bonner,* *Bishop of* London, *sate* first by the Duke her Husband, but the Duke removing her thence, she went and sate by the Bishop, saying, That since she could not sit by him she loved best, she would next him she loved worst: So dear dogged Reader, from writing an Epistle to her I love best, like the Dutchess, I change and remove to you whom I love worst: for Writers hate none so much as Ill-natured Readers: Perhaps you'll ask, why then this Epistle to you whom I hate, and not rather to the Good-natured? Why for the same reason that the Dutchess sate by* Bonner,* meerly to pass my Jest on you; though another may be given, which is, That since Prefaces were partly designed to make the Reader Indulgent and Favourable to the Book he is going to read, there's no need of a Preface to others, since the Good-Natured will be kind to it of themselves; but 'tis you, that put us to the trouble of Prefacing. Therefore to indear it the more to you know, that the main Story is true,* I heard of a Gentleman who was acquainted with the* Irish *Princess, and knew all the Intrigue, and having from him so faithful a Relation of it, I made the Scene the very same where it was transacted, the time the same, going on all the way with the Truth, as far as conveniency would permit; I only added some few Circumstances, and interlined it with two or three other Stories, for variety sake, which is as necessary to the setting off the true Relation, and making it pleasant, especially to you nice Readers, as Sauces are to the dressing up a Dish of Meat, to provoke the sickly Appetite it is design'd for. I Printed it for the ease of her whom it was made for; if you like it, much good may do you; if you will not believe it, you have Liberty of Conscience;* but whether you believe, or disbelieve, like, or dislike, is indifferent to me, since in such a trivial thing as this, I no more fear discredit by writing a bad one, than I could hope for Fame in writing it well. But I believe you are eager to see what is in the Book, and therefore I'll detain you no longer.*

Farewell.

Vertue Rewarded;

OR, THE

IRISH Princess.

As that mighty River* which overflows *Ægypt*, and, with its prevailing Torrent, often drowns those Provinces, which Nature only design'd it to water, yet proceeds at first from such mean beginnings, that most Geographers have been unable to trace it to its Spring:* So Loves swifter and more violent Stream has its first rise from such small Channels, such trifling circumstances, that the Heart it self can scarce perceive its Original; nay very often does not discern its progress, till it is too strong for it, and so the sudden vigour of its Torrent surprizes the unwary Lover, just as the *Zudder* Sea, driven with a North-west Wind, breaks the Diques,* and overwhelms the drowzy *Hollander*,* before he suspects any danger. Yet so Natural is Self-conceit, and so Universal our pretence to Knowledge, that few there are who will be so Modest, as to own themselves wholly Ignorant of any thing which you shall ask them a Reason for. Hence it is, that, among other things, Love too is understood by all, and not one but will give his Verdict of it as soon as you ask him: The States-man will tell you it is caused by want of Ambition; the Merchant for want of Self-Interest; the Souldier for want of Action, and a thirst after Honour; and the Scholar will prove to you, that 'tis gotten by Idleness: But it is with this, as with the Philosophers Stone,* whose mysterious Nature all guess at, and none know what it is, for it very often breaks all the Rules that are prescribed against it: Sets upon the States-man at Court, and overcomes his Ambition; seizes on the Merchant in his Counting-House, and weighs down his Interest; finds the Scholar in his Study, and teaches him a new System of Philosophy which baffles all the old; wounds the daring Souldier, even when he is clad in Steel, and makes him tamely submit to Captivity, in the very midst of his Conquests: The Story that I am going to relate will be an excellent proof of this, being an Instance of an extraordinary sort: It makes Love triumphant at once over two of these his greatest Enemies, the Noise of War, and the Vanity of Ambition; and shows you a Prince of great Valour, guarded equally by both of these, could not defend himself from the Powerful Eyes of a Forreigner, and one as far beneath him in Quality, as Love afterwards placed her above him, when he lay at her Feet imploring her Mercy.

When our present King* had fought the Battel at the *Boyn*,* and drove the Routed Enemy into *Limerick*,* he endeavoured to root up the War, by Reducing that obstinate City, that durst hold out alone against the force of three Kingdoms,* united in a Royal Army; he had then amongst his Forreign Troops* several petty Princes, who fought under him; some as Volunteers, to learn the Art of War under so Great, so Experienced a Master; some as Souldiers of Fortune, who thought by their Valour to recommend themselves to his Favour, and obtain by that means some Important Charge in the Army, the Honour and Profit of which might exalt and maintain them suitable to those High Characters which their Titles deserved. Among the latter sort may be reckon'd the Prince of *S——g*,* the smallness of whose Principality not affording him an Income agreeable to his High Title, and Higher Mind, he was resolved to acquire that Plenty which his Fortune had denied him, and show by his Valour, that he was nothing beholding to her for giving him Titles, but rather that she was unkind, in not giving him as plentiful a Revenue, as suited with the largeness of his Heart, and the vaster extent of his Merit. To this intent he came over Sea in a small Command, if we consider him as a Prince, though in a Post eminent enough to give him some occasions of publishing his Valour; 'twas in this Station he was, when our Forces were from all parts drawing together to invest *Limerick*, in order to which our Prince was to march through *Clonmell*,* a City in the County of *Tipperary*, scituated in a large Plain near the

Sewer, now grown obscure, formerly famous for the great Battel* fought just by it, between two Brothers who were Competitors for the Crown of *Mounster*; when that famous Island had five Crowned Heads to Govern its Inhabitants.*

It was the Chief Street*of this Town our Prince was marching through, on Horse-back, at the Head of his Men, bowing low to both sides, which were fill'd all along with People, who crowded thither to see those Arms which were to secure them from the Enemies of their Liberty and Religion;* when lifting up his Eyes towards the Windows, which were fill'd with the chief Gentry of the City, he espied in one of them a Beauty which fixed his sight, as if she alone were worthy his Attention: He continued looking that way, and turned not his Eyes off the Window, till the fieryness of his Horse (which could not indure to stand still) had carried him beyond the House, and left the delightful Prospect behind him; and afterwards he was so wholly taken up with the thoughts of what he had seen, that he rode on without regarding which way, till one of his Officers rode up, and told him that his Highness was past the House which was designed him for his Lodging: The P. at this began to recollect himself, and giving Orders concerning the good Behaviour of his Souldiers, gave them leave to repair to their several Quarters, whilst he by the Head Officers was Conducted to his; after some Ceremonies past they repaired to their rest, and left the Prince at liberty to take as much of his, as the inquietude of his Thoughts would permit him. He found himself tired with Travelling, and desirous of rest, yet incapable of taking any: He found his Thoughts much disorder'd, and went to Bed to see whether Sleep would compose them: His Soul, like the Bodies of those that have the Rheumatism, seemed very weary; yet as their Limbs are still uneasie, though on the softest Beds, so was his Mind; and coveted sleep as much as their Limbs do rest, and could as little obtain it.

O Love, thou most dangerous Distemper of the Soul! most dangerous because we do not perceive Thee, till Thou art too far gone to be cured: Thou subtle Enemy! who takest the strongest Hearts, because Thou always usest Surprise; and undermining our Reason, never appearest in the light, till Thou art too far enter'd to be driven out: 'Twas thus, Treacherous Deity, Thou didst overcome our Prince, by attacking him when he least was aware of Thee; he little feared Hostility in a Town which he enter'd as a Friend; nor did he expect that one, and that of the weaker Sex, should offer him Violence at the head of his Battalion. He suspected the true Cause so little, that he wonder'd at his own inquietude, and could not imagine what it was that could keep him awake on a soft Bed, who used to sleep so sound in the Camp on a hard Quilt,* and often on the Ground: However, awake he lay all night, and did not once close his Eyes, till day-light shone in at his Window.

At the Sun's first appearance he got up, quite weary of his Bed, where he had the worst Nights rest he ever took in his Life; for though he had indured the hardship of many a cold night in Winter Camps; yet they all seemed easie and pleasant, in comparison of this one Night's Fatigue; for all the thoughts in those Camps of Blood and War, the dread of a neighbour-ing Enemy, and the next day's Battel, were not so troublesome to his Repose, as those of his coming into this Town: The whole Scene of his entrance intruded into his Thoughts; the Noise and Hurry of the People was still in his Ears; and the Window, and the Charming Spectator that looked out of it, seemed still before his Eyes: Though he scarce mistrusted that it was gone so far with him, as to be in Love; yet he was very desirous to come in Company with that beautiful Stranger, who had been so much in his Thoughts, and to satisfie himself whether she was really so Lovely, as she appeared at a distance: But neither knowing her Name, nor the place where she lived, he imagined that nothing but accident could bring him to a second sight of her; but as he was musing upon the difficulty of finding her out, *Celadon*,* the Gentleman of his Horse, came to bid him Good-morrow, and acquainted him, That two or three great Officers were below, waiting for admittance to speak with him: The Prince, who was glad of any thing that might be an amusement to his troubled Mind, sent for them up, and received them with a great deal of Civility: After the first Complements, the Prince told them, He had Orders to await the King's coming to the Town;* and after some discourse of the Progress of Affairs in general, they began to talk of the pleasure of Company, and how they should spend those few days which they were to pass in the Town.

One proposed Training the Souldiers, another the Tavern, and the third a Consort of Musick; and when every one had past their Votes, the Prince bad *Celadon* give his: This *Celadon* was a young brisk *English* Cavalier, of a small Stature, but a Soul sufficiently Great, and which disdain'd to think that the littleness of his Body made him inferior to any one, either in open Valour in the Field, or the management of an Intrigue at home: And certainly never was any ones Humour more equally divided, between Love and War, than his: He was an exact Volunteer in both, and as he would hazard his Person any time, and fight for him that would give him the best Promotion, so was he no less a Souldier of Fortune in Love than War; would change his side often, offer his Service to every Lady that would accept of it, and still was most hers, who was readiest to reward him: He was the Younger Brother of a good Family;* and having gone into Forreign Camps for a Livelihood, he had by his Courage, Wit, and Good Fortune, raised himself so high into the Prince's favour, as to be made his Gentleman of Horse; he being to speak in his turn, told the Prince, That since they had left him a deciding Vote, he was for trying each of them by turns; and if they would begin with the Musick first, he would add to it one of his own most delighting Divertisements, the Company of Women; and to that purpose, if the Prince pleased to be that Night at the Ball, he would take care to invite all the young Gentry of the Town to it: The Prince told him he was the same he always thought him; that *Celadon* that took Love to be as important an Affair of Life, as either Eating or Drinking, and accordingly provided for it as carefully; this raillery brought on other discourse, which lasted while *Celadon* went to make preparations for the Ball; at last he came back and told them that all things were ready, and the Company invited.

On one side of the Town stood a large Country House, which though not built after the *Dorick* Order,* or the exacter neatness of Courtly Lodgings, yet its largeness gave liberty to guess at the Magnificence and Hospitality of the Owner: It belonged to the Great *Moracho*,* famous all over the Kingdom for his Riches, particularly in his flocks of Sheep, as numerous as those of the mighty *Scythian*, whose Son was the Terror of the World;* or that Rich Man of the East, whom the *Turkish* Chronicles make Steward to *Alexander* the Great:* All his Ground, far and near, was thick covered with his fleecy Wealth: You would have thought by their bleatings that you were in *Arcadia*,* and Shepherdism coming in fashion again: 'Twas this House which was pitched upon for the Ball; and what place so fit for Dancing and innocent Mirth, as a spacious Hall, whose Building, Size, and Furniture, altogether rustical, imprinted such lively Idea's of Country Freedom, and Country Innocence: Hither *Celadon* conducted our Prince and his Martial Company; their Musick was as good as the Town could afford, and their Reception suitable to the Riches and Hospitality of him that entertain'd them.

The Prince, who went thither, rather to shun his former thoughts, than out of any inclination to the Company, or the Dancing, sat by, a Looker-on: Some of the Officers who were not so seriously bent, took out those whose Face, Meen,* or Shape pleased them the best, and in their several Dances either shewed their Skill, or at least pleased themselves with the conceit that they did so. *Celadon*, who always employed such a time as this well, was not idle now; but gazed on one, talked to another, bowed to the third, and left none of the Ladies unregarded; and as a cunning Hound, when he comes among a Herd of Deer, singles out the best, and never changes Scent, till he runs him down, so our skillful Hunter, who knew all the Mazes, Turnings, and Doublings in the course of Love, ranged through all the Company of the fairer Sex, till he lighted on the handsomest. He would not leave her, till he had prevailed with her to be his Partner in a Country Dance; and tho' till she was drawn out few observed her, because either Chance, or her own Modesty had placed her in a dark part of the Room, yet when she came into the light, she alone drew the admiration of all the Men, as she did the envy of the Women: Her face was oval and somewhat thin, as if grief had but newly left it, yet her looks were as chearful, as if it had not left the least impression on her mind; some signs of the Small-pox* were just perceivable, yet they and her thinness, instead of lessening, served rather to increase the repute of her Beauty, while they shew'd how it had triumphed over those two great destroyers of the handsomest Faces: Her Forehead was high and smooth, as if no Frown had ever deformed it to a wrinkle; and as much beyond the whiteness of the rest of her Sex, as theirs is beyond the browner Complexion of ours; her Neck, and all the parts of her Face were equally Snowy, except her Cheeks; but they, as if they received their colour from the Rays which her Eyes darted down on them, were of such a lively Carnation,* as if that and the rest of her Face were at a strife, which of those two Colours were the best. Her Eyes were of the same azure of the clearest Summer Skyes, and, like them too, so shining, that it would dazle you to look on them, and her Brows, which grew over them in an exact Arch, were inclining to a light colour, as if they got it from the brightness of those Beams which shone from beneath them. Her Stature* was neither so low as that Sex usually is, nor so tall as to seem too masculine; her Shape was curiously slender, and all her Limbs after a feminine delicacy, but she had withall a Deportment so Great and so Majestick, that the comeliness of the stronger Sex was mixed with the graces of the weaker: And that the stateliness of her Carriage seemed to command that Love and Adoration, which the sweetness of her Face did invite to.

I will not describe how she was drest, let those Ladies be set off with such helps, who like Peacocks owe their Pride to their Feathers; hers were no part of her Beauty, they were put on for Modesty, not for Ornament; and served her as Clouds do the Sun, to screen her more glorious Beauties from the Eyes of weak Mankind, who would else be as infallibly ruined by the sight of the one, as by the excessive heat of the other. The Prince, who sate looking on the Dance, no sooner saw her, but he knew her to be the same whom he had seen in the Window, and whom he so much longed to come acquainted with, he was overjoy'd that he had gotten an opportunity he so little expected; he was so eager to speak to her, and so impatient till the Dance was over, that any one who had observed him might easily have perceived it: As soon as the Dance was ended, he call'd to *Celadon*, and telling him that he could not but be weary, proffered to supply his place: *Celadon*, with a great deal of submission told him, that he was willing to resign any place to his Highness, and so sate down: In the mean time a Tune began, and the Lady waited for her Partner; but when she saw the Prince come, she blush'd, and desired his Highness would pardon her, if she pray'd him to chuse another, because she was weary: The Prince would not allow of that excuse; but when she Danced several times wrong, and put the Company out, and was out of Countenance her self, he thought her blushing proceeded from her not understanding the Dance, and so accepted the excuse, and sate down with her.

Having a mind to discourse with her, and not having so good a command of the *English* Tongue, he spoke to her in *French*, and asked her, did she understand him? she answered him again in the same Language: 'Sir, I have just such a smattering of it as you have of *English*, but your Highness shows me so wise a President,* of not venturing to discourse in a Language which I cannot express my self well in, that I ought to follow it, and dare no more speak *French* to your Highness, than you will *English* to me'. 'Madam, *said the Prince*, though you speak the *French* Tongue so prettily, that one does not know which becomes your Mouth better, that, or your own, yet e're a one of them is thrown away on you; for that tempting Face speaks so much of it self, that had Nature ty'd up your Tongue, yet your Looks alone have power enough to lead all Mankind astray, and draw them more attractively after you by their Eyes, than the most perswading Eloquence can by the Ears'. 'Sir, *replyed the Lady*, Had your Highness made these Compliments to some celebrated Beauty, custom would have prepared her an Answer; but to one that is so unused to them as I am, they come so unexpected, that I must desist Discoursing, as I did just now from Dancing, not so much because I am weary of it, as because I do not know how to go on; and really, with us Country Maids, our Tongues walk like our Feet, and as our Country Dances follow an easie methodical way, so does our Talk; whilst your Court Wit, like your dances, are so made up of Art in one place, a cunning Jest, or a hard Step in another; your Fancies, like your Feet, do caper so high, and are so nimble, that our plainness seems ridiculous in both, and yours is so difficult to us, that it gives us no hope of ever arriving to as much as a faint imitation'. 'Dancing, *said the Prince*, was design'd in imitation of Courtship, the Ladies flying off from the Man to shew her Coyness; her sometimes coming forward, and sometimes retiring, her Inconstancy; and their meeting at last signifies their Marriage; now if the Fashion be here as 'tis in our Country, to kiss at last, i'faith, Madam, I'll leave Poets and Dancing-Masters to shew their Skill in Talking and Dancing, and care not how unskillfully I go on in either, so that I may be sure of my reward in the end'. 'If you go no farther than a bare kiss, *replyed the Lady smiling*, few would refuse your Highness that reward, to have the honour of Dancing with you; but if you carry on the Simile so far as to relate to Marriage, your Highness should consider, that the sport of Courtship, like that of Dancing, is quite gone when it comes to the kiss; and no more pleasure remains afterwards to the poor tired Dancers, than that of thinking it over again; for then, as an old saying of ours has it, our dancing days are gone':* As she spoke these words, the Dance ended, and some of the

Company coming up to hearken to their discourse, the Lady rose from her Seat, and took her leave; the Prince could neither persuade her to stay, nor to give him leave to wait on her home; then he desired to know where she lived, but she begg'd his Pardon: The Prince, who was resolved to know her, sent his Page to observe her, and to take notice where she lodged, and so fell in talk with the other Company, continuing it with one or other, till the lateness of the night broke up the Ball, and sent every one to his several home.

The Prince had not been long at his, e're the Page came and brought him word, that he had housed the Lady in the High-street,* that she lived there with a Gentlewoman who was her Mother-in-law:* The Prince who was so uneasie before, and so desirous to see her, since he had that interview he wished for, began to be more at ease, though more in Love than before, and whereas his thoughts were formerly distracted several ways, now they ran all on her; the Ball, the Dancing, and all the rest of the Entertainment was as faintly remembred, as if he had only seen them in a Dream; but what she had said or done, was as fresh, as if it were that very moment acting over again: One while he fancied he saw her Dancing, another, that he saw with what a grace she spake, and every word of her discourse was as ready in his memory, as if they were the only ones engraven there; no wonder if those who will not give credit to the Stories of Apparitions, say, the Persons are deluded by the excess of Fear, and the strength of their own Fancies, for the force of imagination is as strong in Love as it is in Fear, and makes the cheated Amourist still think he sees the Fair one, and though she be an hundred mile off, yet her Face, her Ayr, her Meen, and every thing that formerly pleased his sight, seems still to dance before it: And as the guilty Conscience of the Murderer presents the Fantom of the Murdered to his view, so Lovers are haunted with Spectres too, only the Murderers appear in a dreadful, the Lovers in a pleasing Form.

This Night had our Prince several of these delightful Visions, which were so intruding, that neither his Reason could banish them while he was awake, nor Sleep free him from them in his Dreams; as soon as he waked he sent for *Celadon*, and having ordered him to shut the Door, and sit down on his Bed-side, he spake thus to him. 'When you went with me to the Emperour's Court,* do you remember how many excellent Beauties we saw there? What variety too, Black, Brown, and Light, yet all fair to Perfection; you may remember how indifferent I was to them all, that I never threw away an hours discourse on them, unless it were to rally the Pride, the Hypocrisie, the Ambition, and the other Vanities which that Sex is given to; and then though I seem'd in Jest, yet I took what I spake to be truth, nor did I think that the low opinion I had of Woman-kind would ever let me shew them any regard beyond bare Complaisance: But I was deceived, for I have in these two days had a greater alteration in my humour, than I believed my whole life could produce'. 'By your words, Sir, I should guess, said *Celadon*, that you are in Love, but the consideration of the place where we are corrects that thought, since in this Island* there is scarce one worthy your high Affections'. 'I wish you could perswade me to that, *reply'd the Prince*; but will not you recant your own Opinion, when I recall to your mind the Beautiful Partner you last Night danced with?' 'The young Gentlewoman, *reply'd he*, had as large a stock of Beauty, as the most Romantick Lover can either wish or imagine in a Mistress; and indeed, if your Highness has a mind to Intrigue away this Winter that's coming on, I could not wish you a pleasanter than she is likely to make, if her Wit be answerable to her Beauty'. 'By what small tryal I have had of her, *answered the Prince*, I believe it falls very little short of it; and if my Love for her encreases a little longer, at the same rate as it has done since its birth, I fear 'twill out-live more Campaigns with me, than I shall Winters with her'. 'Why sure, *said* Celadon, your Highness does not design any more than a Jest in't; for though her Person deserves a higher station in the World, yet, since Fortune has given her neither Quality nor Riches suitable to it, you are not so prodigal a Lover as *Mark*

*Anthony** was, to quit your Principality, and your Honour besides, for a Mistress'. 'There's no need of that, *said the Prince*; don't lay such Blockadoes* in my way to her; for be it ever so long, or difficult, I will use both Patience and Diligence to overcome it; for some way or other I am resolved to enjoy her; and if you will assist me, I shall not think all that ever I can do for you will make you too large a recompense'. 'Your Highness, *said* Celadon, never yet gave me an opportunity to shew my diligence in serving you; but if you please to tell me how you intend to bring this about, I will follow your directions to the utmost of my Power'. 'All that I would desire of you at present, *said the Prince*, is to make me an *English* Song, because I am not well enough acquainted with the Tongue; make it to the Tune we heard sung to Count *Epithalamium*,* and with your Violin and my Guittar we'll go this Night and Serenade her'. 'I'll take my leave of you now, *said* Celadon, and in the Afternoon I'll wait on you with the Song'.

Celadon fail'd not his promise, but came in the Evening, and sat drinking with the Prince till Mid-night, and then they sallied out, to go to the place where they meant to Serenade, taking the Prince's Page with them, both to carry their Instruments, and shew them the House. When they were come under the Window, they play'd a while in Consort, till they thought they had awaken'd those of the House, and then the Prince bad *Celadon* give over, and setting his Guittar to answer his Voice, with a passionate Air he sang this Song,

*W*HY *should my fair Enchantress sleep**
 And yet not dream at all of those,
Whom Love of her in torment keep,
 And hinders from the least repose:
She has kindled fires in my breast,
 Which keep me still awake,
And robs her Lover of that rest,
 Which she her self does take.

When he had Sung thus far he heard the Casement open, and one whisper out of it: 'Who are you that distrust your own Person and Wit so much, that you make your Court by Musick, to help out the one; and chuse Mid-night for the time to pay your visits in, that Darkness may conceal the defects of the other?' The Prince (because 'twas a Woman's Voice, and because he would willingly have it so) concluded that it was his Mistress, and therefore answered her: '*Those, Madam, who have such Beauty as yours to plead with, ought in their own defence to come in the dark, because in the light, the sight of you would take up so much of their thoughts; that when they have most need of them, to express the greatness of their passion, they'd then be at the greatest loss what to say*'. 'You little think how much you are in the right (said she) *for could you see me 'twould spoil your Complementing; for there's nothing so much a bugbear to Wit as an ugly Face*'. Saying this she clapt to the Window, and nothing which the Prince could afterwards say gain'd any return. He, thinking his Sport over for that Night, looked about for *Celadon*, but no *Celadon* to be found, nor could the Page give any tydings of him: The Prince thought he might be gone home before him, and therefore followed him, in expectation to know how he came to leave him, and to tell him of his Discourse with the Lady.

Here perhaps the Reader may charge *Celadon* with Incivility, in running home before the Prince, when he had promised to keep him company; but let the hasty Censurer have as much patience as the Prince himself, who did not expect to see *Celadon*, till he got to his Lodging, and when he came there, was as far to seek for him as ever; but the next morning, the first who came into his Chamber was *Celadon*, his Complexion was wan, and looked as if he was much out of order: The Prince, who guessed he had been upon an Amour, asked him, what made him look so ill. 'After having begg'd your Highness's Pardon', *said he*, 'for my rudeness in leaving you, I'll tell such an accident which befell me since, that your Highness will think a sufficient punishment for it: While you were Singing, I saw at a little distance something, which, by the whiteness, I guessed to be either a Ghost, or a Woman, and as I am not afraid of either, my Curiosity prompted me to see which it was, I walked that way, and found it to be, not a Ghost, but which was worse, a Shee-Devil in a Night-rail,* by which I concluded it to be of that Sex which I had most incli-nation to keep company with at that time of Night; the place too seemed to favour the Temptation, being an old Abby,* where there was no body nigh to interrupt us: When I came near her, she broke silence first, and said, "*O Lord, Sir, you have staid very long, I have been waiting for you this hour*": Tho' at first, by her standing there, I thought her Common,* yet these words made me take her for some Lover who had made an Assignation; I was resolved to personate him whom the meet-ing was designed for; and lest she should know my Voice, I answer'd in a low tone, that business hinder'd me, but I would soon make amends for my absence'.

Just as he spoke this last word, he runs to the Chamber-door, and having seized a Maid of the House, he hall'd* her in, crying out, '*This is the Jilt* that play'd me the trick, but I'll be revenged on her*'. The Maid half dead with fear, could say noth-ing for her self, but cry'd to the Prince for help; he seeing her gentilely drest,* and thinking 'twas his Landlord's Daughter, interposed his Authority, and ordering the Door to be shut, commanded *Celadon* to be calmer, till he enquired into the matter, and asked the Stranger whether she knew what was the reason of his Anger: The Maid desiring that his Highness would hear her, and then judge between them, began thus.

'I perceive by this Gentleman's Anger, that he has been grosly abused; that I have been in some sort the cause, I am sorry; but to shew you I am a very innocent one, I'll give you a relation of some passages of my life, which though publickly known, yet never should have been told you by me, were it not on such an important account as this, the allaying this Gentleman's rage against me, and the hindering him from nois-ing any thing abroad, which might be to the prejudice of my Reputation: My Father is a Country Gentleman, descended from a good Family, but his Ancestors were so improvident, as to spend most of their Estate, and leave him but a small remainder to maintain a great many Children: I am the youngest of all, the Favourite both of Father and Mother, whose greatest care has been to Match me so, that they may live to see me happy. I had choice enough; for these three or four years I have had little rest from Suitors, who from all parts of the Country sollicited me: My Fortune, I believe, they did not court me for, because I saw several who had far greater were neglected; People flatter'd me indeed with the title of a Beauty, and Fame, who is most commonly a great Lyar,* did list my Name among her wonders; whether she was in the wrong or no, I could wish she were, for it has put me to more trouble than a good Face is worth, to bear with the several impertinencies of my young Country Servants; though to have seen their several humours would have been as good as a Comedy to me, had I been meerly a Spectator, but I lost the pleasure because I was an Actress in it my self: Every one of them had a particular behaviour, yet every one something of the *Harlequin** in it; and their Courtship was different, according to their diversity of humours: One had Confidence, and thought that would gain me, and he'd be the most trouble-some, because he'd touze me and hale* me about, and I had much ado to defend my self from his rudeness; him I avoided as I would the Devil. Another would think to gain me by his over-civility, and he'd come a great way just to ask me how I did, and how my Father and Mother did, ask me what a Clock it was, and what time of the Moon, and where I was at Church last *Sunday*; and after some such wise discourse, he'd take a kiss and be gone; he was my Chip in Porridge,* I neither shunn'd his Company, nor cared for it. A third, pufft up with the good success of having gotten his Father's Maid, or Tenant's Daughter with Child, believed the same Methods would con-quer me, and therefore thought to entertain me with immod-est discourse; my Vertue made me deaf to all he could say, and for my Reputation sake I avoided him. Then a Widower came, a Cousen, addressed to me, desiring to be nearer a-kin, and thought to touch my heart, but indeavoured it after so rude a manner, as if he forgot that 'twas a Maid, not a Widow, he was Courting: But it appeared, for all his long practising Merchandise, that he did not understand how to Purchase, for all that he had in the World could not buy my consent to give him mine. A fifth was opinionative of his rustick valour, and he'd aim at conquering his Mistress the same way as Knights Errant did of old, by quarrelling and beating every one he came near: But I thought such an over-boyling Courage, which would still expose me to fears for him, was fitter for a Bravo,* than a Husband. The sixth was my true Country Courtier, who was all Innocence; he had scarce Courage enough to keep him from swooning, when he came into my Company, unless his Spirits had been raised before-hand, by a dram of the Bottle, or a belly full of strong drink; then he'd say, his Mother sent him to ask me whether I'd have him; and tell me a long story of his Ground, his Dairy, and his Cattle; I despised this Milksop, and thought it a hard bargain to give my self in subjection to the chief Beast, only to be Mistress of the rest.

This was my condition, when a young Gentleman, a Stranger, came down into our Country to some Friends he had there; and no sooner saw me, than he encreased the number of my Captives, and professed himself my Servant, but when he first told it me, 'twas with all the Rhetorick which an ingenious passion could invent, his Eyes, his Actions, and every gesture so gracefully seconded his Story, that the Lover's part, which the others acted so ridiculously, became him so well, as if he were only made for Love. When he paid a visit, if any of the rest chanced to come at the same time, the Breeding which he brought from *Dublin*,* elevated him so far above them, in his Discourse, his Carriage, and all he did, that they did look like our wild *Irish** to him; but when alone he talked to me of Love, the Musick of his Tongue was so enchanting, I could have staid and listen'd for ever to him. Sir, I will say no more in his commendation, for methinks Lovers are so much a part

of our selves, that their praises look fulsome where they come
from one another, I will only tell your Highness that we were
but too happy in one another, till Fortune, who is never con-
stantly kind, contrived a way to part us asunder: But why
should we curse our ill Fortune, or lay the fault on the Devil,
when any mischance does befall us? Whereas poor *Beelzebub**
is wrong'd, for he could not do us half the mischiefs we
receive, unless we helped him against one another, and of all
people I think the Envious are his principal Agents, of which
this is a remarkable instance.

There lived in the same House with him, one *Capella**, a
stale Maid, of a good Family, but a decayed Fortune, and she, it
seems, hearing of our Amour, envied the happiness of it: I can't
say 'twas out of any violent Love to him, for her being pretty far
advanced in years, and sickly besides, do make me think her
Loving time was past, at least I'm sure it should have been, for
her grey Hairs, her Dwarfishness, her Sickliness, her Pale Ill-
favoured Face, and her want of a Fortune to gild all these
Imperfections, might have hindered her from thinking of
Marriage, if she had any Wit to consider them; but she will
repent the want of it, when the foolish desire of Intriguing in
her old Age, has rendered her ridiculous to all the Gentlemen,
and after wasting her Youth in Pride and Disdain of those that
more than deserved her, make her take up at last, for want of a
better, with a Ploughman, a Groom, or a Footman. I fear your
Highness will think this a very illnatur'd Character, but I will
beg you to consider, that it proceeds from her own deserts, and
the resentment an injured Love does usually raise in our Breasts,
against those who are the chief causes of our unhappiness; as
certainly she was of mine, for the Nets she often, and in vain,
spread for others, were now laid for him: And because she
thought the Love of me diverted him; after having with Jeers
and Perswasions, Scorn and Flattery, Anger and Kindness, and all
the different ways she could think on, in vain attempted to shake
his Constancy; she was resolved to make me lose him, though
she lost him her self by it; and getting some of her Relations to

represent me to his, as disadvantageously as they could, they (lest he should loiter away his Youth in Love, and not pursue that Preferment to which his Genius was likely to raise him) called him up to *Dublin*. I, partly to hush the discourse which her Malice had raised of us, about the Countrey, partly, because it made me melancholly, to see those deserted Shades, where I had formerly been so happy, quitted that place, and chose my Aunt's House, where your Highness is, now, for my retirement. He came to Town, *incognito*,* to see me, and for fear some of his Friends should hear of it, our meetings were always in private.

An Abbey* hard by (being solitary and free from any company that might disturb us) we pitched upon for our last nights Assignation: I was there first, and this Gentleman coming by, I mistook him for the other: He'll own himself that he began to be too familiar, and lest he should offer me violence at that time of night, when no body was near to help me, I was driven to this shift to get rid of him: I saw which way his nature inclined him, and thence concluded there was no way to deliver my self, but by putting him in hopes of some better Intrigue; I therefore told him, I would not detain him from my Mistress's Embraces, who had been waiting for him this long while (pretending I mistook him for some other Gentleman) and so drew him from thence, designing at the first House I saw any up, to pretend she was there, and so leave him: I durst not come home with him, lest the vexation of finding himself deceiv'd, should make him raise the House, and to come home with an Officer at that time of Night, would have ruined me in my Aunt's good opinion. It fell out as well as I could wish, for an Ale-house was open, and desiring him to go and enquire for her there, I bad him good night, and came home as fast as my fear could carry me: What became of him after I know not, only desire that he would impute it to his own Curiosity, if he has suffered; and that both your Highness and he will be so honourable, as to keep what I have related from others Ears, as strictly as I would have kept it from yours, had I not been constrained to reveal it in justification of mine Honour'.

The Prince, who had listened with delight to the Love-story, it jumping* so well with the humour he was then in, told the young Gentlewoman, that he had a great respect for her, as she was a Gentlewoman, and so near a Relation of his Landladies, but more, as she was Beautiful, Vertuous, and a Lover, and wished her a great deal of Success. *Celadon* begg'd a thousand pardons for the rudeness his Ignorance had betray'd him to; and that she might be the more inclined to pardon him, he desired her to stay, and hear the unlucky adventure he had after she left him. The Prince desired her to seat her self, and *Celadon* with half a smile, and a blush together, thus continued his Story.

'You may remember, Madam, that I promised you to make amends for my long stay, and went about to be as good as my word, had not your Vertue and Cunning restrained me more than my own: And tho' I have all along said that no Woman could resist Opportunity and Importunity, yet now I renounce my Error, and could my self become a Proselyte to Chastity, were I so happy as the Gentleman you waited for, I mean, in having so Fair, so Vertuous a Mistress, to regulate my wandering desires, and confine them to her self; as it is, your example, and last nights trick put upon me, have half Converted me: I will own to you, that I did really think you had mistaken me for another; I was big with hopes of the Bliss you promised to conduct me to; and 'twas either your wisdom, or good luck, not to go into the light with me; I saw indeed so much of you, as to know you again by your Cloaths; but had I seen that alluring Face, your feigned Mistress had not served your turn; I did not, because I avoided your seeing mine, for fear you should discover me to be the wrong Person: For the same reason, I was loath to ask your Mistress's Name, and chose rather to enquire for her at a venture, concluding, that if I once came into her Company, the fear of my discovering her Amour would over-awe her, and make her as kind to me, as if I were the Spark* that she waited for: Besides, the heat of my Inclination pushed me forward at a venture, whether I suc-

ceeded or no: I went therefore into the House, and asked a
Boy at the Bar, whether there was ever a Gentlewoman there
who expected me: The Boy asked me what her Name was:
"*What's that to you*", said I? "*Is there ever a Gentlewoman in the
House?*" The Boy, who understood his Trade, guessed what I
meant; shewed me a Room, and sent in a Woman to me: Her
colour was very good, for I believe she was Painted, her Look
was brisk, and her Garb gentile enough; for my Garb being
pretty rich, they thought to make a good Prize of me, and
therefore sent me, I suppose, the choicest Girl in the House.

I took her to be the distressed Wife of some old Man, who
had married her to make her his Nurse, and therefore told her
it belong'd to my Profession to help the distressed. She told me
she thought, by my Tone and Whiskers that I was an Out-
landish Man;* asked me how long I had been in Town, and
whether I was a meer stranger to that place; pretending as if she
was afraid of my coming to the knowledge of whose Wife she
was. I told her I was an *English-man*, had been beyond Sea
several years; that I came to Town but two or three days ago,
with the Prince's Troops, and should suddenly be marching to
*Limerick,** and that therefore she should make the better use of
me while I staid, and never fear a discovery afterwards; by this
she guessed I should never be able to find the House again; and
that embolden'd them to deal as they did with me; she seemed
to be so cautious, out of a fear of her Honour; when therefore
she had gotten as much knowledge of my being a Stranger, as
satisfied her fears, she began to be more familiar with me, and,
out of a particular piece of kindness, would needs send out for
a Bottle of Sack* for me, saying, she would drink a health to the
good man at home; we both laugh'd at the conceit; I, how little
he thought of his Horns, and she to think how little I suspected
the Trick she was going to play me: The Wine she would needs
drink mull'd, and, ordering it her self, she infused either Opiate,
or some such Soporiferous draught; we had no sooner drank it
off, than she consented to go to Bed, saying, that her Husband
was out of Town, and the House belonging to a Friend of hers,

no body was likely to trouble our pleasures: Because I suspected nothing, I never minded how little she drank; and you know, Madam, we usually indulge Women their liberty in drinking, therefore very likely she drank less, and so it might have less operation upon her; it worked so on me, that I did not wake till late in the morning, and when I first opened my Eyes, I found my self in the innermost part of the Abby, which I saw you at last Night; I was laid on a Tombstone, by the side of a great Marble Statue (the Effigies of some Great Person formerly buried there) I wonder'd to find that my Bed and Bedfellow had both suffered such a Niobetick* alteration, that they who were so soft and warm last Night, were become so hard and cold by Morning; but I wonder'd more at my self, when I found no Cloaths, but an old *Franciscan** Habit on me, I began to think of *Plato*'s transmigration,* and that I had died an Officer, and for my lewdness in my former body, was doom'd now to be an abstinent *Franciscan*.

But I had not much time to think, for by this time, a zealous Neighbour that had seen me asleep, thought he would catch the Frier napping, and brought a Constable for me; the Man of Authority order'd me immediately to appear before a Justice of Peace. I was conducted in State through the Streets, at the head of a Party, more numerous than your Highness's body of Souldiers; they huzza'd all the way, as if the King were going by; and methought I went in great Pomp, only my Triumph was after the *Roman* fashion, with the Lictor* behind me, who every now and then threat'ned me with Bridewell, the Stocks, and the Gibbet:* In this manner I marched near half a mile to the Justice's, barefooted all the way, which I think of it self was sufficient pennance for my last nights Debauch: The Justice asked me a great many impertinent questions; as how I durst appear there in that Habit? and why I did not go after the *French** to *Limerick*? I saw it best to confess what I was, and told him all the latter part of my adventure, how that the People of the House knowing, by my own confession, that I was a Stranger, and not likely to find the House again, had robb'd me

of all my Cloaths at Mid-night, and left me there in an old
Habit, which some poor Holy Brother had formerly given
them as the return of a kindness: The Justice would not believe
but this was a Jesuitical evasion* of mine, and therefore bad me,
if I was a Souldier, send for some body that I was acquainted
with; I named two or three Officers of my Acquaintance, and
the Justice sent one for them, they were found in a Tavern
with a great deal of other Company, and the fellow delivering
his Message publickly, they all came to see the Novice in his
Habit; their Testimony released me, and I was fain to borrow
some Cloaths to go home in, having lost a very good Suit of
my own, and most part of the ready Money I have in the
World, and have got nothing for it, but the name of *Celadon*
the *Franciscan*, which will stick by me as long as I live: Your
Highness may see now the cause of my paleness, is the potion
I drank, and the cold Lodging I had, which if it had not happen'd at such a hot time of the year, would have made me dye
in a more Religious Habit than ever I lived in. You, Madam,
if you have any such thing as pity in you, will excuse me, and
think that the shame, the loss, and the cold I suffered might be
sufficient cause to make me angry with you, whilst I thought
you one of the Accomplices'. The fair Stranger, with a pitying
smile, told him, That she was sorry he had suffered so much by
her means, and said, that to shew she did no way consent to it,
she would send one who should shew him the House; and if
he would carry a Constable with him, he might recover all his
things again.

The Prince, who had laughed till he was weary, bad
Celadon call up the Centry,* him he sent for a File of Musquet-
eers, and desiring the beautiful Stranger to send a Guide with
them to the House, sent *Celadon* with them. The young
Gentlewoman, bidding the Prince good morrow, went to her
Uncle and Aunt to give them some share of the Laughter, and
ordering one of the Servants to go with the Souldiers to the
House, there *Celadon* found his last nights Mistress, and having
recovered his Cloaths and his Watch, he sent for the same

Constable, who had conducted him so carefully to the Justice's, and leaving his Mistress, and her fellow Nuns to the publick Justice, he came back to the Prince very well satisfied that he had come off so well, and bought his experience so cheap.

Though the oddness of *Celadon's* adventure did for some time employ the Prince's mind, yet at last, by a long chain of thought, he returned to the accustomed Subject his Mistress: For as the *Jack of the Lanthorn** is said to lead the benighted Country-man about, and makes him tread many a weary step in fruitless rounds, yet leaves him near the same place where it found him at first; so Love's deluding fire, after enticing the blinded mind through many restless thoughts, brings it about again to its beloved Idea, that enchanting circle it can never leave; 'twas this bewitching Passion which brought our Prince from *Celadon's* adventure to the fair Strangers, and from hers to his own; and when he call'd to mind the Story of her Lover, and his success over her heart, he pleased himself with hopes of the like Fortune in his own Amour, and thought it very probable, that a Prince, who had several advantages over one of a private Fortune, might expect the same success, and not fear the like disappointment, since he had no power to over-awe, or check his Love, or Relations to controul it.

Finding a great deal of diversion in this melancholly entertainment, he resolved on a walk, as well to take the Air, as to prevent the engaging himself in any Company, which might come to seek him at his Lodgings; when he had walked about half a mile, he found himself on the top of a Hill, whence after having looked a while on the adjacent Town, and with a curious Eye searched out that part of it, which his admired Beauty made happy with her presence, he laid him down under the shade of two or three large Trees, whose spreading Boughs nature had woven so close together, that neither the heat of the Sun, nor storm of the fiercest Wind could violate the pleasant shade, which was made as a general defence, no less against the scorching of the one, than the nipping of the other; they seemed to have been first planted there, for the shelter of those who came thither to drink; for just by there bubbled up a clear and plentiful Spring* of which, from an ancient *Irish* Chronicle,* let me give you this Story.

Cluaneesha,* the only Child of *Macbuain*,* King of *Munster*, was accused of having been too familiar with one of her Father's Courtiers; the Fact was attested upon Oath by two Gentlemen that waited on the King's Person, and to confirm it, the Princess her self had such a swelling in her, that few doubted but their Witness was true, and would soon be proved by her being brought to Bed: Her Father, being old and sickly, was desired, for the prevention of Civil Wars after his Death, to nominate a Successour: The People shewed their unanimous consent to confer the Crown on her Uncle, because they would not have a Strumpet for their Sovereign; so the old King was perswaded to proclaim his Brother Heir Apparent, and condemn his Daughter to a Cloister: The Courtier fled beyond Sea, and went a Pilgrimage to the Saint at *Posnanie*;* the very night that he arrived there, one appeared to the Mother Abbess, in the form of a Nun glorified, and told her, that she was *Edith*,* Daughter formerly to King — but now in happiness; that she loved Chastity and Innocence while she was on Earth, and therefore defended it still; that she was constrained to leave the seat of Bliss to protect Vertue, injured in the Person of *Cluaneesha*; that the Persons who swore against her were suborn'd; that the swelling of her Belly was but a Disease; and that if she and the witnesses would go and drink of a Well, which sprung out of a Hill near *Clonmell*, there she would convince all the Spectators, that what she now told her was true: The Abbess told this the next day to the King's Confessor, and he told it the King; the King ordered one who was Confessor to the two Witnesses, to enjoin them, for their next pennance, to drink no other Liquor, but the Water of this Well, for a Week together; they obey'd him, but it was their last, for it made them swell as if they were poisoned; in the mean time the Mother Abbess came down thither with her Royal Novice. She charged them with the Perjury, and they confessed publickly, that the King's Brother, taking the advantage of that swelling, which he thought was but a Tympany,* suborned them to swear against her Chastity, expecting that either it would kill her, or at least it might deceive the People so long till the King was dead, and he in possession of the Crown: A certain Citizen of *Clonmell*, who came among the rest to see them dying, and heard the Confession, admiring the strange virtue of the Water, went immediately home to his Wife, and telling her that he was suspitious of her Honesty, and desired that, to satisfie his Jealousie, she would drink a draught of Water, and wish it might be her last, if she were unfaithful: She not having yet heard of the others punishment, and willing to clear her self, drank of it as he desired, but swell'd with it as the others did, and dyed soon after in great torment.

When the Well had grown famous by the exemplary deaths of the Perjured Witnesses, and the Adulterate Citizen, the Princess declared she would drink of it too; and that the clearing of her self might be as publick as her accusation was, she sent up to the King, who was then at *Cork*, to desire that her Uncle himself might be present when she drank, to witness her innocence; he excused himself, and would not go, but a great many of the Court coming thither to see the Princess clear her self, she went in solemn Procession barefoot, from the City to the Well; and taking up a glass full of the Water, she protested her Innocence, and using the same imprecation with the others, if she did not speak the truth, drank it off; but instead of working the same effect on her, it in a little time cured her of the Disease she had, recovered her Health, and with it brought her so much Beauty, that all the neighbouring Princes were Rivals for her: She had design'd to build a Nunnery by that Well, but her Father dying left her the cares of a Crown, which diverted her from it: But the Well was long after reverenced, and for the quality it had of discovering Unchastity, it was much resorted to; for the Inhabitants of *Ireland* (how barbarous soever the partial Chronicles of other Nations report 'em) were too nice in Amour to take a polluted

Wife to their Bed,* as long as this Well would shew them which was a chast one; but the wickedness of after-times grew too guilty to bear with such Tryals; thence by disuse this Well lost its Fame, and perhaps its Vertue.

And now I will no longer tell such Tales, but leave the uncertain Lover to take his Lot as it comes. Pretty near this Well the Prince lay down, and being pleased with the murmuring of its Stream running down a descent of the Hill, that, and his want of Sleep the night before, tempted him to take it now; *Morpheus** was ready at his call, and waving his Leaden Rod over him, lull'd all his Senses, till a greater power than he rescued him from sleep, to Charm him in a more prevailing manner; for as he waked he heard one hemm, and found it was in order to Sing, for presently the unknown, with a ravishing Air, began this Song.

> Yield, Souldier, yield, give up your Sword,*
>   And don't rebel in vain,
> Yield on all conquering Beauty's word,
> And take what quarter she'll afford,
>   And you shall wear the lighter Chain.
>
> Why do you put such trust in Art?
>   In vain, fond Wretch, you Arm,
> And think Steel proof 'gainst Beauty's dart,
> Which will, like light'ning, pierce your Heart,
>   Yet do your Coat of Mail no harm.

The excellency of the Voice, and the suitableness of the Sence to his own condition, made him lye still to hearken to her that Sung it, and listening very attentively, he over-heard another Voice, which breaking silence began thus. 'I thank you, dear *Marinda*,* for the Song, I like the Tune you have put to it, and either that, and the sweetness of your Voice, do make me partial, or else the Song is very good: I like the Authority it carries with it, for I am usually well pleased when I hear those

Songs, which attribute so much power to our Sex; but prethee
tell me, why is a Souldier the aim of it? when I have heard you
say, that a Souldier should be your last choice, because they are
always abroad, and therefore very seldom enjoy'd after
Marriage, and while they are Suitors their Pride makes them the
most troublesome, and the most inconstant of any; when they
pay a visit, if there be a Glass in the Room, they look more on
themselves, than on her they came to see, and as often as they
look on their Scarf and Feather, their Vanity puffs them up so,
that if we yield not immediately, they Swear and Curse, and so
fall off, taking it as an unpardonable affront that we don't
admire them at first sight; and when they are beloved, their
Self-conceit makes them place it to the account of their own
Merits, and so they value our Love the less, because they think
it their due; nay, and are not contented with a single Conquest,
be it ever so fine a one, and as they do not fight for Malice, so
neither do they court for Love, but out of the pure vainglory of
Conquering; and take as much Pride in having abundance of
Mistresses, as abundance of Soldiers to follow them'.

'You observe right (*said she who was called* Marinda) I'le
grant to you, that for these considerations, they are both the
worst of Servants, and worst of Husbands, and yet in a brave
Souldier there is something so Noble, I mean in his not fearing
dangers, and his patient endurance of all manner of hardships,
that were it not for the aforemention'd inconveniencies of
Absence, Pride, and Inconstancy, I should have a greater value
for such a one, than ever I yet had for any other Employment'.
'Nay, now *Marinda* (*reply'd the other*) you make good the
Character which our Sex bears among the Men, of being
inconstant as the Wind; for 'twas but two or three days ago
you were of a clear contrary Opinion, and you knew the same
qualities of Courage and Hardiness to be then in a Souldier
which you do now, and therefore they are no just reasons why
you should alter your mind; they make some shew of being
Arguments indeed, but I have observed that Wits, when they
alter their Opinions, whether it be in point of Religion,

Allegiance, or any thing else, never want something to say in their own defence'.

'Well, since you are so desirous (*said* Marinda) to know the cause of this alteration of humour in me, I'll tell it you; though in doing so, I rather follow the dictates of Friendship than Discretion, and prove kinder to you than to my self, in telling you that which I am almost ashamed to think of. You know that about three or four days ago a Party of Foreigners made their entrance into this Town, with the Prince of S——g at the head of them, Curiosity made me open my Window to see them pass by, either the desire of looking about him, or the pride of being gazed at, made the Prince ride slower by that place than ordinary, and he had his design, for I looked as stedfastly on him, as if he had been the only Pageant there; and tho', without doubt, there were several Officers very brave* and fine; yet the seeing him first had so prejudiced me in favour of him, that I could not think the rest worth the looking on; all the rest of that day I could not forbear thinking of him, fancying I saw with what a Grace he sat his Horse, how stately he look'd, so far beyond the rest of his Souldiers, as if nature, as well as Fortune, had marked him out for a Prince and distinguished him from the rest, as much by his person, as by his power; and as the thoughts of the day have an effect upon those at night, so I believe these were the cause of my being disturbed in my Bed with this Dream. The Prince, methought, in my absence, had hidden himself in my Bedchamber, and, when I came in, started out upon me: He had on one side of him a little wing'd Archer,* who bent his Bow, and aimed at me several times; but just by me there started up a great Gigantick form, with no other Arms but a Shield, and he, methought, still interposed that, and with it kept off the Arrows of the other; at length, methought, the Prince spoke something which tempted my Defender over to his side, and left me to the Mercy of the young Archer, who shot me through and through; and at the same instant the Prince came and catched me in his Arms, and told me I was his Prisoner, at which, methought, I swooned away with a pleasing pain, and at the fright of it I awaked. People say Dreams are significant, if they are, tell me what you think is the meaning of this?'

'Why truly, (*said the other*) any one who should hear you tell this, might guess, without any great skill in Fortune telling, that you are in Love'. 'If (*said* Marinda) I did think a little the day before upon the Prince, which might have been the cause (*as you say*) of this Dream, yet those thoughts were too slightly grounded to be of any long continuance, and I was in hopes in a day or two to have clearly rooted them out; and the next Afternoon one of my Acquaintance came to desire my Company to a Ball, I was ready enough to accept of the proffer, because I imagined that the Musick and the Company would cure me of my thoughtfulness; but (as my ill Fate would have it) it was clear contrary; for whom should I meet at the Ball but the Prince; you were there, and saw how I was clearly put out of my Dance, with the confusion his presence put me in: He sate down with me, and made me some few Compliments, which tho', perhaps, were coveted by some of the Company, yet had those Ladies seen my inside, as well as they did my out-side, they would rather have pitied, than envied me; 'twas he that sung under my Window last night, and though you mis-took him for your Servant, yet I knew his deluding Voice too well: His words were so pathetical, and the Tune so moving, that though he had skill enough at the Guittar, which he plaid on, yet that kept not time with his Voice truer than my Pulse and Heart did'.

'Have a care Marinda (*said the other*) that you do not engage too far with one who is so much above you; 'tis not safe Intriguing with Persons of his Quality; Inferiour Lovers may be jested with as long as we please, and thrown off at will, but such as he seldom leave us without carrying away our Vertue, or at least our Reputation: And you will too late curse your own Charms when they have exposed you to be ruined (like a young Conjurer) by raising a Spirit which you are not able to lay'. 'I fear (*reply'd* Marinda) he has spy'd something in my

behaviour that (he fancied) favoured him, as Mens conceited-
ness makes them too apt to discover such things; I am sorry for
it, if I did discover any weakness in my self, that should
encourage him to such an attempt: I am sure my Tongue never
dropt the least word in his favour; and if my tell-tale Eyes, or
my Countenance has betray'd me, I'll disfigure this Countenance, and tear out these Eyes, rather than they shall invite, or
assist any enterprize, to the prejudice of my Vertue'.

Now though I have told the Reader the discourse these
Ladies had in private, yet let him not expect that I shall tell him
the Prince's thoughts upon it; that I should not be able to do,
though I had been in his heart, for they were so different, that
he scarce knew what to make of them himself: He certainly had
need of a great presence of mind, to resolve upon such a sudden
what to do, whether to discover himself, or no: If he did, he
saw some probability that the Lady might be kinder, when she
knew that he had heard her confessing a Love for him; if he did
not interrupt them, he thought he might hear more; but while
he was in this irresolution he chanced to Sneeze, at which the
Ladies arose from the seat which they were on by the Well, and
walked away, very likely because they found some body was
nearer than they had imagined, and were afraid of being over-
heard in their discourse: The Prince lay a while musing on what
he had heard, and then went home; he related it all to *Celadon*,
and asked his advice what use he should make of it: *Celadon* told
him it was not the safest way to extort a confession of Love
from her, by letting her know he had over-heard her, because
that might make her angry at his hearkening, and such a
discovery might be too violent for a Maiden Modesty, and so
nice* a one as hers seemed to be; he desired him rather to
continue his Addresses, and so bring her by degrees to a
voluntary submission; that this was the more natural and the
surer way; that twice or thrice more being in her Company
would ensure his Conquest over her; and what need was there
to hazard her displeasure, by forcing her to confess she loved
him, when he was well enough satisfied of it already?

The Prince consented to this, and contrived this way to see her; he knew the Town was so full of Souldiers, that every House had some of them in it, he thought hers quartered some Officers, and enquiring out who they were, he told *Celadon* that he would go and see them at their Lodgings: That Evening they went together to the House, and a Maid shewing them into the Parlour, they found there *Marinda* and two Strangers, one of which the Prince knew to be the same he had seen at the Well with her; they would have left the Room when they saw the Prince come in, but he was too well skill'd in War to let a weak Enemy retreat, he had not sought her out to let her go so easily; he was thinking of some shift to put off the Officers, whom the Maid was gone to call, when to his great satisfaction she brought him word, they were not at home: He said, that having so pleasing Company, he could very well stay till they came in, and sitting down, he made a sign to *Celadon* to entertain the Strangers, to give him the greater freedom with *Marinda*, and that he had not long, for the Mother came in: Then she (as old Women usually do) took up most of the talk her self, till the Prince, tired with it, took his leave.

As they walked home, *Celadon* asked the Prince what he thought of *Marinda*. 'I take her, (*said the Prince*) to be the most perfect Innocence that ever was since the fall of *Eve*:* Her words are so Witty, and yet so modest, her humour so nicely Vertuous, and yet so Civil, that I account the Country Ignorance which is in her, to be beyond all the breeding in the World. I told her that I made an advantagious exchange in getting her Company, by their not being within whom I came to see; she said, she was not of the same opinion, since if Men in general were as good Company as I, she must needs blame the unkindness of Nature, which had made her of so unsociable a Sex, that she was neither Wit enough to converse with Men, nor would the Rules of Vertue give a Maid that liberty, if she were otherwise qualified for it: I told her that all who knew her but so much as I did, must needs contradict her, in that Nature had given her Wit as well as Beauty; that the one was made to delight the Ears of Men, the other their Eyes; and as without always closetting her self up, she could not bar us from the last, so neither, without great injustice, could she deprive us of the one half of our happiness, by tying her self up to an obstinate silence, meerly to deprive us of the other. She smiled, and said, she had not power enough over her self, to observe that silence* which a Maid ought; but that since Men, by their insinuating discourse, drew words from her which she should keep in, she would shun the Company of that deluding Sex, and so keep her self from yielding so much to them, by not coming within reach of the temptation: She blushed as she spoke these words, and I might have gained ground mightily on her yielding heart, if the old Gentlewoman had not unfortunately come in to her rescue'.

The prince pleased himself much with the thoughts of his Conquest, but he knew not what a stubborn Enemy Vertue is, and how difficult it would be for him to take any advantage over a Heart, which that maintain'd against him. Having found so little resistance at his first visit, he believed *Celadon*'s observation was true, that two or three more would win her; he went often, under pretence of seeing the Officers, and sometimes met with them, but never with *Marinda*; once or twice the Servants said she was abroad,* but the last time he enquired for her, they said she was sick; he fancied that she had ordered the Servants to deny her, and therefore judged the readiest way to see her would be by his former Stratagem, a Ball; and that he might not be expected there, he gave out the Evening before, that he was going for *Dublin* the next day to get Orders from the King: He rode through the Town that Morning, and her House being in the way, he called at the Door, and asked to speak with one of the Officers that lodged there, but to the intent that she might take notice where he was going: When he was out of sight of the Town, he rode back again to his Lodgings another way, keeping close, that no body might know of his return; and when he thought the Ball was at the highest, he and *Celadon* went there together; the place where they Danced was the same where the first Ball was, the Company almost the same, only that it wanted the Beautiful *Marinda*, but in wanting her it wanted all, nothing there was worthy to entertain our Prince, therefore he called to *Celadon* to go with him home; but *Celadon* was of another mind, he was not so nice in his choice, to retire himself from such variety of good Company, meerly for the absence of one; he was very little pleased with the capriciousness of the Prince's humour, and would have willingly staid behind, if he had thought it would not disoblige him.

But the Prince being desirous to go, they took leave of the Company, and were going out together, when, at the Door, they were met by a couple of Ladies in a strange *Spanish* dress; and their Faces, after the mode of that Nation, had long Vails over them: *Celadon* bobb'd* the Prince, and desired him to come back to see what Masks those were, telling him, that under them he might chance to find *Marinda*; the Prince was in hopes of it too, and made up to them, but found himself deceived; for speaking to one of them in *French*, she seemed not to understand him, but whispered to the other, and she spoke to him in *Spanish*, asking him whether he was not the Prince of S——g, Commander of the Forces now in Town? The Prince answer'd her that he was; but desired her if she could speak any other language to do it, for he understood very little of that. 'I speak, Sir, (*said she*) a little *English*, and if your Highness can understand me better in that, I shall beg the honour of a hearing from you, for I do not know but it may lye in your Highness power to do me a great kindness'. 'What is that kindness, pretty Petitioner (*said* Celadon) for all your excellent counterfeiting (Madam) I fancy you are two of this Town, that pretend some sober business with us now, and design to laugh at us when ye are gone, for being so little curious, as to see nothing of a Lady but her dress'. 'That you may not think (*said the other Lady in broken* English) that we are not of this Countrey, we'll dance you a Sarabrand* after the *Spanish* way, and if that will not convince you, I can shew you so ugly a Face, that mine shall be the last Veil you shall ever desire to look under'. 'Let us have the Dance (*said* Celadon) and if your Air and Meen be as becoming as your Shape, I shall venture to look in your Faces, for all your threatning'.

The Company left off Dancing to look at these two, whose dress seem'd so extraordinary, and the Prince, who had a mind to see them Dance, ordered the Musick to play such a Tune as pleased them best, and they with their Castinets acquitted themselves very gracefully, and came off with the commendation of all the Company: Their Shapes and Carriage being very near alike, *Celadon* did not know which to like best of them; he told them that now he must desire to see their Faces, that the handsomest might take him all to her self, and free him from the double Captivity he now lay under, of being a Slave to them both; but one of them told him they could not grant it, for she had a boon to the Prince, in the begging of which she must open such private passages of her Life, as would make her ashamed to be seen by the Man that knew them; but if it e're lay in the Prince's power to grant her it, then she would turn *English* Woman, and throw off her Veil. The Prince said that was a very plausible excuse, and desired *Celadon* to urge the Strangers no more, and turning to them, told them, that whomsoever that Story concerned, he desired she would tell him, and he would, according to her directions, serve her to the utmost of his power. Both the Strangers gave him a very low Courtesie, in token of their thankfulness; and one of them desiring the patience of his Highness, and the rest of the Company, seating her self in the midst of them who had left their dancing to listen to her, she began thus,

The Story of Faniaca.*

PERHAPS this Company, and more particularly that part of it which is of my own Sex, may censure this freedom in me, and think it too much openness in a Maid, to discover things of such privacy in a publick audience, which the rest of Woman-kind make their Closet-secrets; but my *Spanish* Mistress, upon this very occasion, told me a Story of a *Spartan* Boy, who having stolen a young Fox,* and hidden him under his Gown, rather than be discovered, kept him there till he tore out his Bowels: So it is with the *English* Ladies, if once Love enters into their Breasts, though, like that Fox, it prey upon their Hearts, yet out of Modesty they keep it secret; and though the closer it is hid, it gnaws the fiercer, yet, like the poor proud Boy, they hug it to 'em, and conceal it till it ruins them: But the *Spaniards*, and those of my Country, who are in a hotter Clime, tye not themselves up to such cold, such rigid Rules of Honour: Your Love, like your Winter Sun, is so clouded, that those he should shine on are never the better for him; ours is so hot and predominant, that there is nothing can cover him: Now you your selves cannot give a good reason for this nice piece of Modesty, which allows you to take a fancy to a fine Dog, a fine Horse, or any thing else that is handsome, only Man, which is the stateliest, gayest Creature of all, you must not own a regard for: Sure this Tyrannical custom was founded at first by some old decrepid Matrons, that were past the enjoyment of Love themselves; for Nature, that has allowed you the publick freedom of all other pleasures of life, would never consent to disgrace this sweetest of all: Whence comes it then, that tho' most of you are fond of it, yet you manage it so secretly, as if it were Treason to our Sex to own it? While I am in *England* I should dissemble, like the *English*;* but pardon me for once, if I break this general rule, in searching for a Lover, whom I can never find, but by discovering my self wherever I come, that some of those who hear me, may chance to bring the same story to his Ears, that so he may find me again.

My Name is *Faniaca*, my Father was a *Brachman*,* an *Indian* Priest in the Province of *Antis*,* which Countrey having never been conquered by the *Incas*,* kept up the ancient Barbarity,* not being Civilized by their Laws, as those Nations were, who had yielded to their Government: And whereas they with one

[73]

consent worshipped the Sun,* we of *Antis* had several Deities, the two chief of which were the Tyger, and a large Serpent, which we called *Amaru:** To these it was our custom to sacrifice Human Blood; they commonly fed on nothing else but Captives,* and if we had no Captives, we were forced to find them the same sort of Food from among our selves: But we rarely found any such want, for there being an irreconcileable Enmity, first between us and the *Incas,* and then with those *Indians* who took part with the *Spaniards,* we had so frequent Engagements, they to extend their Dominions, and we to defend our own, that scarce a day happened, but brought us in some new Prisoners; for the *Spaniards* had a great Colony at *Cozco,** and from thence they every now and then sent Parties far into our Countrey to take Booties, and make discoveries of the Land, in order to a farther Conquest: These Parties were commonly made up of *Indians,* with *Spaniards* to head them, because they would willingly spare their own Nation, and Conquer ours at the Natives expence.

These *Spaniards* still encroached farther on us, till they had driven us over the *Madalena,** that great River, being very deep, of a strong swift Current, and at that place about a League broad, made it seem as if our differences were now at an end, Nature it self having divided us: On each side of the River there was a considerable Town,* of which, the one was possessed by their Party, the other by ours; and though sometimes our Fishermen would meet by chance and kill, or take one another, yet we never gave one another a troublesome visit on shore, by reason that our Canoes were not big enough to transport Men in so great numbers, as to dare to Land; and it being about 300 Leagues down the Sea, we never had seen, or could imagine any which should hold above ten or twelve men at most; for our Canoes were made all of a piece,* and how to put different Planks together, as Ship-Carpenters do, was an Art wholly unknown to us: Some of the *Spaniards* had taught our Enemies this, and they privately built a great many large Flat-bottoms,* which the Governour of their Town fill'd with *Indians*, and sent a few of his own Countrey-men with them; these Forces he sent over about Mid-night, with orders to Land at our Town, kill all the Men, and sending back the Boats, to keep the Town till he Landed an Army sufficient to fight his way farther into the Country. In this Town my Father lived, and was Priest to the Tiger and an *Amaru*, which were accounted the largest of any thereabouts, and therefore were worshipped the most, and had their Adorers to bring them presents from all parts.

Those *Indians* who took the *Spaniards* part, were always very inveterate against us, because the *Incas* made both their Government and Religion* different from ours; as soon therefore as they entered the Town they kill'd all, without any distinction either of Sex or Age; I was awakened out of my sleep with a dreadful cry, such as you may imagine that of a taken City to be, where their Enemies are so unmerciful: I streight leapt off my Quilt, and ran into my Father's Room, for when by the cry I knew our Enemies to be entered, I expected to lose my Life, and therefore chose to lay it down by him who gave it me: I found him in a great Consternation, and hanging about his Neck, I expected the coming of our Enemies.

The first who entered the Room was a *Spaniard*; for though I had never seen one before, I knew him to be one by his Dress, and a Helmet which he had on as soon as he entered, I left my Father, and fell at his Feet to beg both our Lives; and while I was in that posture, he bade his Souldiers stay back; but one of them cryed out, *This is the Cupay*,* (that is the Devil, or Conjurer) and advancing before the rest, ran at my Father with his Spear; the Commander immediately broke out of my Arms, which were clasped about his Knees, and, drawing a Pistol from under his Girdle, shot the *Indian* dead; and pulling out the other, he turned about to his Men, and swore that the first who disobeyed his Orders, as that Dog had done, he'd teach him what was the Discipline of a Souldier: While they stood all silent, amazed at the speedy Justice he had done on their Country-man, he came to me, who was lying on the Ground bemoaning my Father, whose Blood stained the Floor, he raised me from the Ground, and clapping a Guard of Souldiers on me, (with orders to keep us two from receiving any violence, upon pain of their Lives) he went away, I suppose, to help his Part'ners to take the other parts of the Town: Within an hour after he came back, and pulling a Box out of his Pocket, he took a Plaister out of it, and put it on my Father's wound, and bad me fear nothing; assuring me, that he did not come to destroy us, but to reduce us to a better Government; and as for me, he told me, that if I pleased, he would make me so happy, that I need not fear any danger, either of Poverty, or Captivity, from the alteration of my condition.

This, and the approach of day-light, did somewhat comfort me; my Father came to himself (for loss of blood had made him swoon) and began in the kindest words he could, to give thanks to the preserver of his Life, who was hugging and comforting me, when of a sudden we heard the same confused noise in the Streets, which we heard in the Night: I thought our Enemies were finishing their Cruelties upon their Captives, and could not forbear bursting into Tears at their Miseries: The strange Commander endeavoured to comfort me all that he could, saying, That he could not help what the other Captains did to their Prisoners, but his own, and particularly my Father and I, should have no violence offered us: The noise grew louder and louder, as it drew nearer, when looking out of the Window, we perceived the *Antian* party driving the *Peruvians* before them, and before he could resolve what to do, they were killing his own Souldiers at the Door; he with a great deal of Courage leaped forward, and after all his men were kill'd defended the Door alone; and with his Spear laid the boldest of them dead at his Feet: You will, perhaps, think that I was glad of this change of my Condition, to see my self unexpectedly freed, and my Countrymen revenged of their Enemies; but I'll assure you I was not; the danger which my generous Defender was in, weighed down all the Joy of the other, and though my fear made me for a while stand, as far as I could from the

Weapons; yet, at last my desire to save him, overcame my Cowardise, and running to the door, I placed my self betwixt him and the Spears, which were bent against him; and cryed to my Father to speak to them to let him alone, my Father was so weak with the loss of Blood, that he could not come to the Door, but called to them with all the entreating words he could think on; most of them knew my Father and me, and having a great Veneration for us (as all our Nation has for their Priests) they gave over assaulting him: Only the foremost of them asked me, why I would defend one who was the Enemy both of our Country and Religion; I told them 'twas to him, that both their Priest and I owed our safety; that he kill'd the Man who hurt my Father, and with a great deal of care dressed his Wound; I desired therefore that, for our sakes, they would give me his Life.

These words perswaded them to leave him to me; as soon as they were gone, I went out to see how things went, and brought him word, that a great Party from the Mountains, was come to our assistance, and that all who set foot on our Land were killed: *And, Madam* (said he) *shall I be the only man who goes home, and carries the news of so great a defeat? Or shall it be said, that ever a* Spaniard *let a Woman beg his Life of an* Indian? *Not of one* Indian (said I) *for you were over-powered by numbers: No one but you* (said he) *should have given* Astolfo* *his Life; but since I receive it from you, I'll make that use of it I should by serving you, and revenging my self of my Enemies, for this loss and disgrace I have suffered.* I told him, that since he confessed his Life was mine, and that I had preserved it, it was not generous to use that Life against my Country; however, I left him to his liberty, and promised him, that at Night I would send him over in a Canoe to the other side.

When Night came, I was as good as my word; and calling two trusty Men, I ordered them to row the Stranger over the River, telling them that his presence would be enough to secure them from the danger of their Enemies: At our parting he expressed himself very thankful to me for my generous usage of him, and told me, that e're long he would make me a return, in the mean he desired me to wear that about my Neck, pulling a Gold Medal, with a Chain of the same Metal: I, who had heard of the *Spanish* Covetousness, gave him a large Golden Wedge, and desiring him never to be my Country's Enemy, or put himself into the like danger, I took my leave, and left him to his Fortune, the Men came back before morning, and brought me word that they had set him safe on shore, and that all the other side of the River was covered with Men: This news, which they told about the Town, alarm'd us, and that Party which came down from the Mountains to our assistance, waited to receive them; some of our Scouts, who rowed as near the other side as they durst, brought us word that they had abundance of Canoes fill'd with Men, which made us think they design'd to Land by force, where the others had by Night; but this was but to amuse and draw our Men that way; for they had provided a great number of Planks about 20 mile higher, and having lighted on a place where the River ran between two Hills, and therefore could not extend it self a quarter of a Mile, they made a floating Bridge,* and on that they passed over some Men, before ours knew any thing of it; they took such care to surprize the Natives, that no one came to bring us Intelligence of their being Landed, till some of the Planks which came floating down the River, made us suspect something; we sent some Scouts up the River, to discover what was the matter, and they brought word that the Enmy was on this side of the River: Ours marched towards them as fast as they could to fight them, before any more came over, and having joyned Battel, the first news we heard, was of a great Victory, we had gained over them; and a great many Prisoners brought us, as the proof of its being true.

The *Indian* Prisoners were kept up to feed our Gods; but some few *Spaniards* that were taken, as being the Nobler Captives,* were to be feasted on; as it was our Custom to tye our choice Prisoners to a Tree, and a great Fire being made just by, the Priest was to cut off Slices from the more fleshy parts of them, and distribute them about to the People to broil and eat: If the Captive shewed any signs of pain, or groaned at his Sufferings, we counted him of a base Spirit; and after burning his Body, we scattered his Ashes in the Wind; but if he endured bravely to see his Flesh eaten, we dryed the Sinews and Bones, and hanging them upon the Mountains, we deify'd them, and went Pilgrimages to them. There were ten *Spaniards* brought to my Father, and two or 300 *Indians*, who were all tyed, and secured by a Guard set over them; the *Indians* to be a Prey to the Bellies of our Gods, and the *Spaniards*, to those of our Souldiers: As soon as they were brought in, my Curiosity prompted me to see them, but very little to my satisfaction; for the first I set my Eyes on was he whom I had set at liberty before: I was both concerned and amazed to see him there, and uncertain whether I should do any thing in his favour or no; therefore I pretended not to know him; till he making as low a bow as his being tyed would permit, asked me, did I not know him whose Life I had saved?

'Are you he, *said I,* whom I set free but a few days ago? I thought your good usage might have made you our Friend, or at least your dangerous escape might have been a fair warning to you; but since you are the second time come amongst our Enemies, and are still plotting my destruction, you shall suffer for your ingratitude, and to shew how little I pity you, I will go to see you Sacrificed, and eat the first bit of you my self'. 'As for the danger of coming again (*answered he*) a *Spaniard* fears none, but I was so far from plotting your destruction, that I hung that Medal about your Neck for my Souldiers to know you by; I had indeed a design upon your Countrey; but for you, my greatest desire was, by saving you and your Family, to shew how much I aimed to ingratiate my self into your favour'. 'These are all but Wheedles (*said I*) to save your Life; but they shall not serve'. 'No, they shall not (*said he*) for since you can entertain such mean thoughts as these of me, I scorn to take my Life; all the repentance my attempt has brought upon me is, that it has displeased you; I thought to have requited you for giving me liberty, and to have made you amends for the loss of your Country, by bringing you to a better, but since this ill success has prevented me, all that I desire, is to dye in your favour'. 'The way to do that (*reply'd I*) is to dye undaunted, for then you shall be one of our Gods'. 'I will do so (*said he*) be you there, and shew but the least sign of pity at my death, and I'll go off with such a Courage, that him whom you slighted whilst he was alive, you shall adore when he is dead'.

Though in a Man's mouth who was at liberty, this would have looked like a Boast, yet coming from one who did not know but he might suffer next day, it appear'd so brave, that I could not but admire it: The others held their Tongues, but looked so fierce, as if they kept silence out of disdain: I went thence with a great opinion of their Courage, and a secret horrour in my self at the cruelty of our Nation, which gave brave Men such barbarous usage: I called to mind his professing a design to save me, and carry me to a happier place; and his telling me of the thing about my Neck, for a Token to know me by, made me believe it was true; and when I considered of this, I imagined I ought to save his Life, but I could not tell how to do it without my Father's consent: As I came into the Room where he lay ill of his Wound, there was one brought him word of the death of his only Son; who was found after the Battel among the Slain, with a Bullet lying in him: I shewed my sorrow in all the extravagancies which our Nation commits on the like occasions; but my Father only gave a groan or two, as it were to rouze up his anger, and said, that he would comfort himself for his Son, in revenging his Death, since all his grief could never raise him to Life again: That all the *Spaniards* who were in the Battel were killed, except ten who were in his Custody, and he would sacrifice each of them, because he would be sure that his Sons Murderer should not escape; for since he was killed with a Bullet, he did not doubt but it was a *Spaniard* shot him.

We lay all that Night awake grieving for my Brother, but the next day, when the first Fury of our grief was over, and my

Father began to talk with me about our Prisoners: 'Suppose, Father, (*said I*) the *Spaniard* who saved our Lives should be one of them?' 'If that should come to pass, (*said my Father*) he had better staid where he was, than come over to seek his Death here the second time'. 'But, Sir, (*said I*) gratitude would oblige us to save his Life, who saved ours first'. 'That we have done already (*said my Father*) and so we have returned his kindness; and if after so hard an escape he should be come again, he does not deserve his Life, neither would I be guilty of so much injustice to my Son and my Countrey, as to save that Man's Life, who has been the Death of the one, and has made a second attempt to be the Destruction of the other'.

This arguing of my Fathers seemed so reasonable, and his Indignation so just, that I could not gain say it, and therefore said no more to him, but went back to my Prisoner, and told him, that I did intend to save him, and his Companions for his sake; but that my Brother's Body being found shot, had so incensed my Father, that I could not prevail with him to spare them; and therefore I told them they must prepare their Courage to dye, as soon as my Father's Wounds would suffer him to assist at the Solemnity. 'Well, (*says he*) since I must dye, and it does not lye in your power to help it, I am sorry you told me you attempted it, for that shews so much kindness, that it makes me desirous to live: I was willing to dye when you upbraided me with the begging my life, but now I can no longer be suspected to flatter you out of any such hopes, since you say it is not in your power to help me; I own that my Death is no grievance to me, only as it prevents my living for you; and all that I'll now desire of you, is to let me dye the first, that I may not behold the Cruelties exercised on my Country-men'.

The Love and Courage which I perceived in these words, quite altered the thoughts I had, of giving him up to my Father's resentments; and from that time I found something within me so strong on his side, that it over-ballanced the Duty I should have paid to my Father's will, and my Brother's

Blood: I went to my Father, and told him that he who saved his Life was there, and urged to him how ingrateful we should be, if we did not restore him to his Liberty; but my Father answered me with the same Arguments he had done before: Then I endeavoured to corrupt him that was Captain of the Guard that looked to them, but he was a Blood-thirsty violent natured Man, and not only refused me, but complained to my Father, who was so angry, that I should endeavour to release so many of our worst, our most formidable Enemies, the *Spaniards*, that he threaten'd, the next time I attempted the like, he would have me condemned to suffer with them, as the Enemy of my Country. I knew his violent temper too well to venture any farther, and gave over all hopes of saving my Prisoner: The next morning four *Indians* were to be carried to our Gods to feed upon, they drew Lots for their Lives, they were blind-folded when they drew, and I held the Cistern,* and decided who the Lot fell upon, and it often grieved me to doom the poor trembling Slaves; my Prisoner seeing me picking out some of them for Death, told me, he longed to know when his turn would come; I told him that his must come as well as the rest; that I had incurred my Father's displeasure on his account, and left nothing undone which I thought might be for his safety, that I hoped this was all he could expect, and desired him to own before his Death that I was out of his debt; yet I had resolved with my self to keep him till the last, in hopes that before that time the Guards might be changed, or else my Father's anger might be mitigated, when most of them had been sacrificed to it: Two or three days had now past over, in which time my Father had given the Guards particular charge to beware of the *Spaniards*, for fear I should free them; the day came that he found himself well enough to perform the Sacrifice, and our *Spaniards* were brought out in the midst of their Guards, to draw Lots which of them should make our Banquet; by ill chance it fell on my Prisoner; I changed the Lot, and sentenced one of the others in his stead, but not so cleverly but that my Father perceived it: The poor wretch was cut to pieces slice after slice, and lived long enough to see his own Flesh broiled, and eaten by the Company; you must think this was a terrible sight to the rest, who saw by their Companion what they were to suffer.

I expected to keep him the same way I had the first day, and went on the morrow with the same design, little dreaming what would happen; for my Father, who had seen me play the Jugler the day before, would hold the Pitcher himself, and the first black Lot was again drawn by my Prisoner: Upon that the Fire was made to broil his Flesh, he was stript naked, and tyed to the Tree; he looked about him, without as much as chang-ing Countenance at his Destiny; but when he turned his Eyes towards me he blushed, I believe out of shame, to think that I should see him in that helpless condition: Such a sight as this, which would have drawn pity even from a merciful Enemy; what effect then do you think it had upon one that loved him? Or rather, what effect had it not? I blusht and grew pale, Anger, Love, and Fear, succeeded one another; Anger at the Barbarity of my Countrey-men, Love for him, and Fear at his danger: But just as my Father's Knife fetched Blood from the brawny part of his Arm* (the place which he first began with) I was not able to bear up any longer, but fell in a swoon; which my Father perceiving, left him, and catched me in his Arms; but not having yet recovered strength enough to bear me up, he fell to the Ground with me, and lighting upon his Wound, rubbed the Plaisters off, and made it bleed afresh: My Father was immediately taken up on some of their Shoulders, and car-ried home, and every one said 'twas an unlucky day, and the Gods were angry, so the Sacrifice was deferred till the next.

When I came to my self, I was very glad to see the poor Man delivered from immediate death, though it cost some of my Father's blood, but it almost distracted me, to think what a short reprieve I had for him, only till the next day; his Fate was now at its Crisis, and within twenty four hours I must either see him free, or mangled to pieces; all my former hopes lay in deferring the time till another Guard came, which perhaps I could have bribed off, or till my Father's mind was altered; but his Anger continued still; and because he found the Captain of the Guard as violent against the *Spaniards* as himself, he ordered him to continue in the same Post, till all the *Spaniards* were Sacrificed: My poor Prisoner's Lot was come, and he to dye the next day, and I had not yet thought on any way that could prevent it: After having wracked my Invention a great while, for a way to free him, at last I lighted on this: There were two of my Father's Servants, whom I sent formerly to row my Prisoner over the River; I knew they wished well to him, because when he enter'd our House as an Enemy, he had saved their Lives; these two I acquainted with my design to release him: I gave them a large Pot full of pleasant Liquor, made of our Sacred Plant the *Coca*,* and bade them towards Night to bring that to the Guard-house, as a present from my Father: Our Guard consisted of a hundred Men, for the preservation of the Temple, and the Treasures of it, and the Prisoners who belonged to it; so that all these things might well require the care of an hundred Men: We had near twice the number of *Indian* Prisoners, besides the nine *Spaniards*, only they were Armed, these were naked and tied: Out of the Temple I had got Arms enough for them all, and conveyed them into a Room hard by, to be ready upon occasion; when the two Servants came with the Liquor, all the Souldiers crowded into the Guard-house, only two who stood to their Arms at the Prison Door; when the Servants saw them all engaged about the drink, they left the Guard, and came to give me notice; upon which I took some Daggers (which our Souldiers had taken from the *Spaniards*, and hung up in the Temple as Trophies) these I hid under my Gown, (for the Women of our Nation had thin silk Gowns to wear in the cool of the Night) and so under pretence of seeing the Prisoners, I conveyed these unto them: When I came in I saw my Prisoner asleep, I cut the Cords of his Hands and Legs, and as I cut them he awaked and found himself loose; thence I went to another, and still as I loosened them I put a Dagger in their Hands: I told them I was come to give them all Liberty, if they would shew themselves Men, and Conquer an Enemy whom they would find surprized, and not ready to oppose them. *And my* Astolfo (said I) *I have done all this for your sake, yet I will rather stay behind you, and undergo all the punishments that an angry Father, or incensed Town could inflict upon me, than fly with you, unless you are as willing to receive me, as I to go.*

Several of the *Indians* wept for Joy, and the *Spaniards*, for all their Gravity, could scarce forbear it: My Prisoner said, that he was more glad of my Love, than of the saving his Life, and would have told me abundance of the like nature, had he not been interrupted; for one of the Centinels, not liking my long stay, came to see what was the matter, and no sooner came in but he was stabb'd by one of the *Spaniards*; my two Servants had stood all this while at the Door, and when one of the Centinels left them to come to us, they dispatched the other; by this time the *Indians* had untyed one another, and I carried them to a Chamber hard by, where I had laid the Arms: Some of the Guard, hearing a noise, chanced to come out, and mistrusting something more than ordinary alarm'd the rest, but they came a little of the latest, for we had as many Armed as they; they began a very bloody Engagement, and a great many were killed on both sides, but our number increasing we over-powered them, and they fled every way for safety. My Prisoner had given me in charge to some of the *Indians*, who were formerly under his Command, and they kept me in Rear till the Guard fled: Then *Astolfo* came to me, and desired me to come down to the River side, before the Town Guards came upon us, for our noise had alarm'd the Town; and there were at that time five or six thousand Men which were left with us, for fear those on the other side the River should make another Invasion; but we were too quick for the uproar, before the Guards came we got to the River, and there being abundance of Canoes, and the Enemy coming after us, you may guess we did not stand to Complement who should take Boat first: The eight *Spaniards*, *Astolfo*, the two *Indians* and my self, took the same Canoe: We put off altogether as fast as we could, but in a little time we were parted from the rest, the night being so dark that we knew not which way we went, though the Wind blew so hard from the other side, that we were afraid 'twould force us on our Enemies Coast, to our ruin: Two of our *Spaniards* tugg'd against it as hard as they could, till one of them broke his Oar, and then we gave over striving, and let the Boat go down which way the River would carry it; the next morning we would have made for Shore, but having but one Oar the Wind beat us off, and carried us down all that day and the next night with the Stream.

Though the first day we got away we were very chearful, yet now wanting Provisions, and being driven down we knew not whither, dampt the Joy we should otherwise have taken in our Love and Liberty: I began to reflect on my former actions, and to think this a just punishment for my undutiful leaving my Father, and my Country; I began to grow faint with hunger, and he was so troubled to see me in that condition, that in the greatest danger of his Life I never saw him shew so much sorrow. The farther we Sailed the River still grew wider and wider; on one side we could not Land, because the Wind would not let us, on the other side we durst not, because 'twas inhabited by those Nations who are mortal Enemies to the *Spaniards*: We were now come down a great way, and the River had turned so, that the Wind, which before was against us, now was for us; we made towards the Land with the great-est haste that a violent Hunger could make; as we came near the Shore we discovered a Boat lying under a Rock, we made towards it, and saw only one Man in it, and he was asleep, so that we were upon him before he awaked; he would have resisted, but finding it in vain for one Man to fight with eleven, he yielded up himself and his Boat; in it we found store of Victuals (the richest prize we could have wished for at that time) and you may think we fell on to some purpose: We examined the Fellow, and he said he belonged to a Ship which lay about sixty Leagues lower; that they sent twenty Men up the River in quest of a Prize which they were to take, by plundering a little Town thereabouts; he told us, that there were about so many more left in the Ship, but that the greatest part of them lay sick of the Wounds they had received in a late Engagement: We stept into his Boat, and going down the River, in eight days time we came within sight of the Ship; then having got out of the Man what intelligence we thought necessary, we threw him over-board, and made up to the side of the Pinnace;* it being duskish, and they knowing their own Boat again, they mistook us for their own Men; so that half the *Spaniards* entered, and had killed all that were above Deck, before they mistrusted any thing; the rest they took Prisoners, and (throwing all the Wounded Men into the Sea) because we had not Provisions sufficient to last us all, they set their Prisoners on Shore, and so came down the River merrily in a Ship of our own: The *Spaniards* fell to searching, and found some Bullion in her, besides a vast deal of ready money, which, after a just division between us ten, we computed would amount to near 30000 Ducats a piece, so that with a general consent we Sail'd streight for *Spain*, intending to Land at the first Port of that Kingdom which we came to.

Now we were happy enough, we had escaped our Enemies the *Indians*, and Famine, which had like to have proved a more fatal Enemy than they; besides the Prize which enriched us beyond our expectation, and came in good time to help my needy Fortune, who in that hurry of leaving home, had not remembered to bring any thing of value with me, besides a few Pearl* which I always wore about me. My Servant came and took me in his Arms, congratulating my escape out of the several dangers we had been in, and thanking me a thousand times for the kindness I had shewed in saving his Life; and more for leaving a Father, to run the same Fortune with him: In fine, he promised that he would requite all my kindnesses, by having me Christened, and marrying me as soon as we came to *Spain*: And I was so well pleased with the alteration of my Condition so much for the better, that I think that Night was one of the pleasantest of my Life.

The next Morning we spy'd a Sail making up to us, and as soon as it came within reach, it sent a great Shot to command us to strike Sail; we saw by the bulk that it was a Man of War, too strong for us to resist: We, much against our wills, staid for it, and received some of them on board; in searching our Ship they found divers Colours, as Pyrats usually have; our Vessel, it seems, had been one, and for their Faults who had owned her, we were all seiz'd, our Vessel made a Prize, and our Men taken Prisoners: The Man of War being a *Spaniard*, the Captain said he would reserve *Astolfo* and his eight Country-men to be tryed on Shore, and condemned to the Gallies:* My two *Indians* (notwithstanding all my intreaties for their Lives) he hanged on the Ropes before my Face: But taking compassion on me, he said he would keep me to wait on his Wife: Accordingly, when we came upon the Coasts of *Spain*, he sent the nine *Spaniards* Prisoners to *Sevil*;* and though I begg'd him to let me accompany *Astolfo*, he kept me at Sea a few days more, and then Landed me at *Aveiro*,* and gave me a present to a Wife he had there.

It would be tedious for me to tell you, how ill I bore this worst change of my Fortune; I raged, I grieved, till my Sighs and Tears grew so thick upon one another, that no one could know which was the most plentiful of their two Fountains, my Heart, or my Eyes. My Mistress, who was a good natur'd Gentlewoman, interested her self in my Sorrows, and would often enquire what was the reason of my grieving; till at last her Importunities drew from me the whole Relation, which I have now made to you; she bade me be comforted, and think no more of him; I told her I could not be satisfied without him: *That opinion* (says she) *is, I hope, a false one; you must be comforted either without him, or not at all, for you must never expect to see him again; for supposing he should escape, being condemned to the Gallies, yet how is it likely that you, who are a Stranger, should find out a single Man, and one of no note, in such a large City as* Sevill, *or one who perhaps, before you could get thither, would be gone to some other part of the World?* I told her I had an Art, by which

I could do more than that; and thus much I knew, that if I were at my liberty, and had a little travelling Money, I should not be a year e're I found him. She asked what Art that was: *'Tis what I learned from my Father,* (said I) *and is very common among us:* She desired to see the effects of it; I told her I would shew it, in resolving whatever question she would ask me. She bade me tell her where her Husband was at that time, and when he would come home: I told her she must buy me a small Drum, which had never been used before, and I would then tell her that question, and any other. When she heard me affirm it so confidently, she said she would try me, and bought me a Drum: I that Night used some Charms over it, which my Father and I had practised on such occasions; and the next morning I told her my Master would be at home on the morrow: *I thought* (says she laughing) *how you could foretell: Why your Master is gone into the* Straights* *a cruising, and bade me not expect him these two Months.* I let her enjoy her incredulity, but she had like to have suffered by it; for she, good Woman, considering that her Captain made long stays and short returns, had providently looked out for a Gallant, to comfort her in his absence; but I was yet too much a Stranger to be made acquainted with such privacies.

She had an old *Spanish* Maid, who was the only Servant she kept, till I came; this Maid was privy to all her Intrigues. They had at that time pitched upon a young Gentleman, who had an Estate near the City, he was very fond of my Mistress, as Men usually are of every new Conquest, and had invited her to spend a few days, in her Husband's absence, at his Countrey Seat: She consented to go with him, and they had assigned a day to go together, and as it happened, 'twas the very day after that on which my Master was to come home; but it drawing towards Night, and my Mistress hearing no news of him, nor seeing any likelihood of his coming, she sent her Maid to invite the Gallant to Sup with her; me she sent up to Bed, pretending that she had some business for me to rise very early the next morning: I lay in the Room over her, and though I went to

Bed without the suspition of any such treachery against my Master, yet chance discovered it all to me: I awakened after I thought I had been a pretty while asleep, I fancied I heard a Man's voice in my Mistresses Chamber, and concluded it was my Master's, because I thought my Art would not deceive me; however, my curiosity prompted me to a desire of knowing whether it was he or no: I got out of Bed softly, and looking down, I saw her sitting at Table,* with three dishes of Meat before her; (which in hungry *Spain** is a noble Treat) by her there was seated a fine young Gentleman, he whom I just now described to you; their discourse, at that instant, happened to be of me. She told him she had a Slave who pretended to fore-tell future events; that she had told her that the Captain would be at home that day; the Gentleman laughed, as he said, to think that a Slave should be so bold, to impose such a Story on her Mistress; he laughed at her too, for giving any belief to me; and I laughed at them both, to think how secure they fancied they were from my Eyes and my Masters, and yet how much they were mistaken.

While I was peeping down, and listening to their discourse, we heard a loud knocking at the Door; my Mistress cry'd out immediately that it was the Captain's knock, and that she was undone, unless they could hide him somewhere in that Room; for to send him up to mine, was the way to let me know of it, and being a Stranger, perhaps I might betray him to her Husband. The Gentleman was young and slender; and his Limbs, which seemed composed rather for Love than War, shew'd that he was a very unequal Match for a great two-handed* Sea Captain: And you have all heard enough of the raging *Spanish* Jealousie, to think, that if a young handsome Man had been found there, and at so suspitious a time, 'twould have gone near to have cost all three of them their Lives. The Captain still knocking harder and harder, made them all at their wits end what to do with him; at length they bethought them-selves of a great Chest, which my Master had given his Wife full of Plunder, when he first came on shore with me; but she

had taken all those things out, and my Master had filled it with
Sea Bisket,* which he had bought for his Men; the Mistress
and Maid emptied these Biskets out under the Bed, and begg'd
the Gentleman to try whether he could get into the Chest; the
young Spark was as complying as she could wish him; he made
a quick shift to get in, and his Fear was at that time so strong
upon him, that it would not only have driven him into that,
but into a Mouse-hole, if there had been one in the Room.

As soon as he was in, the Maid let in my Master, who
seemed a little angry that he was kept so long at the door; and
seeing the Cloath laid, and the Table covered with Meat, he
asked my Mistress how all that came there, and what she
designed with it? I wondered how she would come off; but she
very readily answered, that she provided it for him, and kept
him at the Door while she took it from the Fire, that he might
be the more surprized, to find so good a Supper ready for him
on the Table. He asked how she could provide it for him, since
no Man in *Aveiro* knew of his coming? My Mistress answered,
that the *Indian* he had left with her, had told her he would certainly be at home that night. *When did she tell you this?* (said he)
Yesterday (answered my Mistress) *Then, by St.* Jago,* *she is a
Witch,** (said my Master) *for yesterday morning, till the Storm came,
I did not know (that I should come) my self: I hope,* Captain, said my
Mistress, *you have received no damage by the Storm: None,* said he,
*but the spoiling my store of Bisket, which got wet, and my poor Men
are in want of it; but I will have you,* said he (turning to a Cabbin-
Boy that waited on him) *go now and call two or three of our Men
on Shore, that we may have hands enough to carry that Chest of
Bisket to the Water-side: Time enough for that to morrow, Love,* (said
my Mistress) *No,* (says my Master) *my Men are in present want of
it, and I ought to take care of them, as well as of my self.* The Boy
went on his Errand, and my Mistress with a great deal of pain,
waited the unlucky coming of the Seamen to carry the Chest
away, and her Jewel that was in it.

I had till this time been an unconcern'd Spectator, and
only pleased my self with the fright my Master's coming had

put them in, but now I saw I must help them out, or they had no way of their own to bring them off; dressing my self therefore as fast as I could, I went down to them; my Mistress, I believe, wondred to see me there, when she thought I was asleep, yet she did take no publick notice of it, lest my being sent up to Bed, should give my Master the greater cause to suspect something. After bidding my Master wellcome home, I turned to my Mistress: 'And did I not tell you, Madam, (*said I*) that my Master would be at home to Night?' 'You may see, (*said she*) by my preparations for him, that I believed you': I could not forbear smiling to see how she would have imposed on me, as she did on my Master: 'But, Madam, (*answered I*) since I have given you such a proof of my skill, which (though it has told you this only for tryals sake yet) hereafter may shew it self some way, which may prove more serviceable to you, I would desire one favour of you in its behalf': 'What's that? (*answered she*)' ''Tis (*said I*) that you would pardon me for an accident which befell me in the performance of it': 'What's that (*says she*) I hope you have not raised any Spirits that have broken our Windows, or done any damage to the House': 'What if they have (*said my Master*) you shall pardon any slight mischief that they have done': 'They have done no mischief at all, (*said I*) pray do not be affrighted, Madam, and I'll tell you all: When you were abroad yesterday I set about my Enchantment, to answer your question, but you came home a little too soon, while I was asking some questions concerning my own Fortune; hearing you at the Door, and not having time to lay that Spirit which I had raised, I ordered him to throw the Bisket out of the Chest, and enter into it himself;* you can't but have heard how mischievous Spirits are, while they are at liberty, and to prevent any such mischief, I confined him there, till your absence should give me leisure to lay him: You went soon after to Bed, and I durst not tell you how near the Spirit was to you, for fear of fright'ning you, nor would at all, had not the present use my Master has of the Chest, forced me to this discovery'.

When my Mistress heard this told, she ran to my Master, and clasping him about the middle, pretended to be in the greatest fright imaginable; and desired him to leave me the House to my self, till I had ridded the house of the Devil. Though the hot Supper, which my Master believed prepared for him, and my Mistress saying, that 'twas because I foretold his coming, had confirmed him in the belief of my Art; and the earnestness with which I begg'd pardon, made him not question what I said to be true; yet he laughed at the extream fear, which his Wife so excellently counterfeited, and said, 'Never fear, Wife, that Mr. Devil, who has been so civil as to lye there all last night, will be so rude, as to disturb us now: Sure, *Faniaca*, he he will not force us to leave our Victuals to cool, to dance attendance on him: If he will give us leave to Sup, we will retire afterwards, and give you leisure to dismiss him': 'Not for the World, (*said my Mistress*) I cannot eat one bit, nor enjoy my self one minute, while the Devil is so near us; dear Love, consider the danger 'tis to be here, and let us go to some Neighbours, and leave the Witch and the Devil together': 'Since you are so fearful (*said my Master*) have but patience, till my Men come, and I'll order them to carry the Chest up Stairs, for I am loath to leave this hot Supper; but do not shew your fear to them, for if they know that his Devilship is in it, 'tis likely they won't venture to meddle with it.'

My Mistress said, she thought it long till they came; and I dare swear she did not counterfeit in that, but was at that time as desirous to get rid of her inclosed Spark, as ever she was to get into his Company: The Sea-men kept her not long in pain, for they came while we were talking of them: My Master mentioned nothing of the Bisket to them, but desired, before he sat down, that they would remove that Chest up one pair of Stairs for him: Two of them immediately laid hold on two Rings which were fastened in the sides of it, and heaved it by degrees up stairs, I lighting them the way; the Stairs were so narrow that they could not go both on a breast, but one pulled the Chest up, and the other heav'd it after him, by which

means our Gallant was almost stifled in it, for his Head chanced
to lie at that end which was lowermost; therefore, when it was
near the top, he not being able to endure it any longer, stirred
about to lye easier, and coughed; at which the Men, being star-
tled, let go, and the weight of the Chest tumbled it down that
pair of Stairs, and another pair which joined just to it; though
the Chest was locked, yet the tumbling of it made me expect
every moment that it would fly open; and therefore, lest it
should discover the Gentleman, I dropt the Candle: My
Mistress shriek'd at the noise, and clapt too the Room Door
where my Master was; he stood silent, not knowing what to
think of the noise; one of the Seamen stood by me till the
Maid brought us a light, but the other, who bore up the lower
end of the Chest, was driven down all the Stairs before it: I
heard the poor Man groan, and was terribly afraid that it was
the Gentleman's voice, and that the fall had crippled him; I
therefore desired them all to stay in the Room while I went
down Stairs, they were willing to obey me, for the horrid noise
had put them in such a Fright, that they stood gazing one at
another, wondering what the event would be: When I came
down, I found the Chest open, and the Gentleman gone; then
I helped the hurt Man up Stairs; his Head was broken, and
some parts of his Body bruised with the fall, but he was more
afraid than hurt. 'Well, *said my Mistress to me*, this comes of
your raising the Devil'. The Seaman, who did not know what
to make of it before, hearing her say it was the Devil, concluded it was so indeed; and said, He was sure 'twas a cloven
Foot trod on him, for he felt it, and that he saw the Tail of it,
as it went out of the House. 'What, then is he gone (*said my
Mistress*)'. 'Yes, Madam, he is gone (*said I*) and shall trouble you
no more': 'A good riddance (*said she*) of your Mischievous
Spirits, pray raise no more of them': 'Then, Madam, (*said I*)
you must not give me the occasion'.

Now my Mistress's real fear was over, her counterfeit one
vanished with it, and bidding us set Chairs, she and my Master
sat down; the wounded Man he sent on Ship-board to the

Chyrurgeon,* and having supped and diverted himself with the poor imprisoned Devil, they went to Bed, where he passed that night with my Mistress, who would rather have had that Devil for her Bedfellow. The next morning my Mistress's Confessour came to her; and my Master, who was filled with the last nights adventure, could not contain himself from communicating it to the Father, saying, That he had given his Wife an *Indian*, that could raise Spirits, and make them tell her things that were doing at ever so great a distance; relating, withall, what had happened by that means in his House the night before: The Holy Man, stroking up his Beard, with an austere look, told him, that this was no Jest, said, it was making a compact with the Devil, and that his Christianity obliged him to confess himself an Enemy to all such actions; and therefore was bound in Conscience to discover this to the Fathers of the Inquisition;* and desired my Master to secure me: He said this when I was by; I was earnest to know what he meant by the Inquisition; but when he told me the danger of coming under the clutches of that bloody Court, and named some of their Punishments, as the Wheel, Immuring, and other ingenious Cruelties of theirs, I would have given my life for a *Maravedy*.* When my Master was gone out, I fell down on my knees to my Mistress, and begg'd her to give me my liberty, and put me in some way to escape this barbarous tryal, that the Priest would bring me to: I told her I was loath to mention the kindness I had done her, in conveying her Spark away, lest that should look like upbraiding her with it; but thus much I must say of it, that it was that Story which made the Priest so zealous against me, and that if ever I came before the Inquisition, Self-preservation would force the truth from me, and that I must confess the Cheat I put upon my Master, to avoid the imputation of Witchcraft. She answered me very civilly, that she had such a sense of the kindness I had done her, that she would requite it with giving me my freedom; and when my Master came home, she was very urgent till she prevailed with him to do the like; whether she did this out of gratitude to me, or the fear of my threatning a discovery, I do not know; but my Master called me to him, and bade me go and hide my self on board that night, lest the Officers should come to search for me.

The next day he came on board himself, and asked me where I would rather Land, I told him in *England*; for I had consulted my Drum, and was informed, that I should find my Lover in one of the Northern Islands, coming from the Siege of a City,* and the Rumour of the *Hollanders* just then Landing in *England*, made me think that likely to be the place: We met at Sea with an *English* Merchant, and giving me a little Money, he put me on board there; I had, besides, some Money my Mistress gave me at parting, and a Pearl Necklace, with some Bracelets, which my Master (finding so great a Prize with us) spared me, when he plundered me at Sea; these sold in *England* for two hundred Duckets;* with some of this Money I put my self into an *English* Garb, keeping my *Spanish* one by me, and went up to *London*, and hired my self to a Person of Quality; and being an Outlandish Woman,* and appearing in a very gentile Dress, I was made her Gentlewoman; I staid with her near a year, in which time I put up a little more Money, and good Cloaths, and learn'd *English* enough, and then I left her, to travel in quest of my Lover: I went down to *Chester*,* and hearing that there was a War in *Ireland*,* I embarked for this Kingdom; I have been in *Dublin*, and am now come hither to follow the Camp, where I am assured I shall find him: I get as much as maintains me on the Road, by telling Fortunes to the Gentry, who sometimes are very liberal to me: Amongst the different Fates I read, those belonging to Love delight me most, as being most agreeable to my own temper; and when ever it lies in my way to forward any of those by my Skill, my being in their Circumstances, makes me the readier to help them.

She ended thus, to the admiration of all the Company, whose Ears were tyed to the Story: The Prince, who was pleas'd with the Wit of the *Indian*, could not deny her those praises that were due to it; and from her ingenuity in the management of her intrigue, and her constancy in continuing it so long, he concluded that the *Spaniard* must needs be happy in her; and told her, that if he was in the Army, whether he were in Commission, or a private Souldier, he would do what lay in his power to contribute to the finding him out for her, But, he said, he expected a kindness of her in retaliation, and that if he searched for her Lover, she would (if need were) do him the same service; that he never gave any credit to Gypsies, or any other Vagabonds that pretended to her Talent, but since she had proved her Skill in so exemplary a manner, he would lay aside his former incredulity, and desire she would satisfy his Curiosity in some things, which it would conduce to his quiet to know. The *Indian* said, she would wait on his Highness, at his Lodgings, the next day, and give him what satisfaction her Art could afford him. But he was not the only Person that wanted her assistance, neither had the terrours of War so frighten'd Love, as to make him wholly abdicate his power over that Kingdom; but in this Ball he had some Votaries of both Sexes, and the ingenious *Indian* told publickly the place where she Lodged, that those whose Modesty restrained them from speaking to her there, might have a more private opportunity. The Prince went home well satisfied with the hopes of knowing his Fortune, and told *Celadon* that he was so impatient to see the next day, and the *Indian* that would satisfie his Doubts, that he found himself not the least inclinable to Sleep; therefore, if he would make him a Song, in answer to that, which he told him he had over-heard his Mistress singing at the Well, he would that Night go Serenade her with it; and though he could neither meet with her at the Ball, nor find her at home, yet this Song would make a discovery which might alter the reservedness of her Behaviour: *Celadon* made one; about Midnight they sallied out together, and stopping under her Window, the Prince, with the best air which his Guittar and Voice could frame, began this Song, to the same Tune which she had Sung to hers.

*T*HE *Souldier yields his vanquish'd Heart,*
    As Conqu'ring Beauty's prize;
And though he fears no mortal Dart,
    The Thunder of your Frowns he flyes,
And dreads the Lightning of your Eyes.

You shall dread this more, said a Voice interrupting him; the Prince looking about, to see whence the Voice came, saw three naked Swords making towards him: *Celadon* came up immediately to his assistance; it being so dark, that neither Party could see to defend themselves, there had been fair work in a small time, if some of the Guards, walking the round, had not been pretty near them; when they came up, the three fled, and the Souldiers knowing the Prince, Congratulated his Highness's escape, from a Death, which the most unskillful Enemy might have given him, when there was not light enough to allow him fair play for his Life: They would needs wait on him home, and he considering that the noise might have allarm'd some of the Neighbours, thought it best to retire, for fear of raising a discourse, which might prove prejudicial to his Mistress, and offend her.

The next Afternoon the two Strangers came to wait on the Prince, and finding him alone, one of them told him, she was come to make good her promise, that she brought her Companion with her, who understood nothing but *Spanish*; however, if his Highness had any secret extraordinary to communicate to her, she would go with him to another end of the Room; the Prince opening a Closet Door, retired in thither with her, and opened his mind in these words: 'Since I want such advice, as cannot rightly be given, without some foreknowledge of what will be the issue of it, and since my business is nothing but an Amour, who so fit to consult about it as you, who are a Fortune-teller, and a Lover too? You may understand then, that my business is nothing but Love; it is one so violent, and yet so unreasonable, that I am unable to curb it, nor have I any hopes of success, if I let it go on; and 'tis just with me now, as with a Souldier, whom his too boyling Valour has engaged so far in the Battel, that his Enemies have surrounded him; there's no retreating for him, because the Foe is behind, nor any likelihood of breaking through, because there are too many before him: So am I surrounded with difficulties, pushed forward by Love, and opposed by Despair; carried on by her Charms, and driven back by her Disdain; now I would know what my success may be, if I go on, and accordingly I will either nourish this Passion, or tear it from my Breast?'. 'I cannot see, (*said the* Indian) what should discourage your Highness from proceeding, since there are those perfections in your Highness, which give you desert enough to pretend to the best of Women: I fancy your Highness has fallen in Love with some one below you, and that your Love and Ambition are at variance, whether that shall draw Love up, or Love draw that down: I know these two generally tend two contrary ways, that one, like Earth, descending, the other, like Fire, still aspiring upwards'. 'You guess as right, (*said the Prince*) as if you had seen my Heart; and if you can tell me how I shall succeed in my Love, I'll make that, or my Ambition, conform it self to the other: I doat on one who is beneath me; when I made my first Addresses, she seemed Pliant enough, as if she had no aversion to my Love; nay, I over-heard her once confessing to a Confident, that she had a kindness for me; and when I thought her my own, I found my self most deceived; for some Capricio* or other made her, that she would never since admit me into her Company; I went several times to enquire for her at home, but the Servant still shifted me off, either denying her, or pretending she was sick; I contrived last Night's Ball, in hopes to entice her thither, but it failed; I Serenaded her last Night with a Song, in answer to one I heard her Sing, that time she confessed a Love for me, but before it was ended, I was interrupted by some Night Adventurer, who attempted to kill me, which makes me suspect 'tis some Rival; inform me by your Art, whether this is a Favourite that supplants me in her Heart, or whether it be Virgin Niceness,

Hypocritical Modesty, or what else it is that has put this sudden stop to my Success?' 'This is a puzzling question (*said the Indian*) but give me one Night's time to consult my Drum about it, and I will bring you an answer'.

The Prince seemed well contented, and the two Strangers, taking their leaves of him, left him to expect the insight the next day would give him of his Fortune. On the morrow they came again, and the Prince took the *Indian* into the Closet (as he had done the day before) and desired her to be as plain as she could, in foretelling him all that was to befall him in his Love: 'First, (*said she*) your Highness must acquaint me whether you design Marriage, or no'. 'Marriage! (*said the Prince*) why did not I confess to you, that she was a private Gentlewoman, one beneath me? I wonder you should ask such a question': 'Pray, Sir, be not angry, (*reply'd the* Indian) for how can I tell your Highness what success you are like to have in any design, until I know the design it self?' 'If (*answer'd he*) I can enjoy her on any terms, but those of Marriage, I shall think my self very happy; if not, my Love has not so wholly blinded me, as to make me forget my Interest, and my Honour'. 'Your Highness (*said she*) is certainly very prudent, in having so great a command over your Love; and pray make use of it, when I shall tell you the state of your Affairs: The Lady you Love, has a Gentleman who loves her as violently as you, only a more honourable way: Your Highness's Fortune has altogether the ascendant over his, if you are inclined to lay hold of that advantage, if not, my Art tells me, that, within a Week, she will be too far off for you to enjoy, or ever to see her again'. 'And is this all the hopes you can give me? (*said the Prince*)': 'Yes, (*said she*) only thus much I may add, that your Fortune promises you a great deal of happiness, if ever you have her; but if you Love, I need not tell you this, for Love injoy'd is always happy; since, if there be such a thing as happiness, it is to be in that condition which is most delightful to us; being in possession of what we Love,* is being in the condition which is most delightful to us, and thence may well pretend to be the highest of Enjoyments'.

'I see you are so Indulgent (*said the Prince*) as to humour me in my Love, but that is destructive to me, and therefore we'll talk of it no more; there's something (*said he*) by way of gratification, for the trouble I have put you to': The *Indian* told him, she would not receive any such reward, for the unwelcome news she had brought him; that all the requital she desired, was his Highness's favour to the *Spaniard*, if ever she found him: Only desired his Highness to take her advice, never to put himself to the trouble of another attempt on his Mistress, unless 'twas with a design of Marriage, for her Art declared it would prove unsuccessful: That if his Highness ever wanted her help in this, or any other business, he might find her in this Town, where she resolved to stay, till the Army was marched through it to *Limerick*, because that was the likeliest way to find out her Lover.

With these words she took her leave, and taking her Companion with her, left the Prince in the greatest distraction of thought imaginable: The assurance which the *Indian* had given him, that he must expect no success, unless in a Vertuous Love, made him resolve to shake off the mean Passion; but all his endeavours were vain; the more he tryed it, the more sensible he grew, how unable he was to perform it: He advised with *Celadon*, and they agreed to carry on the Intrigue, in spight of what the *Indian* foretold; and this agreed best with the Prince's humour, who, though he could not entertain the thoughts of Marrying her, could less endure the thoughts of losing her. They contrived to have it thought about Town, that *Celadon* had fallen into the Prince's displeasure; the Prince shewed the first signs of it in the House, and they of the House soon reported it abroad; *Celadon*, with a seeming discontent, left the Prince, and went to Lodge with one of the Officers, at *Marinda*'s Mother's.

There was a young Gentlewoman, a Cousin of *Marinda*'s, and her chief Confident, the same whom the Prince had heard talking with her at the Well, the only comfort of her Parents, who were worth above ten thousand Ducats, of which, their

Deaths would leave her the entire Possessour; she was withal very Witty, and good Humoured; but Nature and Fortune, who not often agree to be over-kind to the same person, had here followed their usual Custom, making her want in Beauty, what she had in Riches: And as her Wit was keen, and sharp, upon all that came into her Company, so Nature had given you an exact Copy of her inside, by her out-side; for her Face had as much of Satyr in it, as her Tongue; the Chin of it was sharp and long, the Nose tucked up, as if it fled from her Mouth, which was so wide, as if Nature had designed it for some Cormorant* Body: Her Face was all over studded with Freckles, which, like the Stars in the milky way, lay so thick, that you would have thought it one continued yellowness; only her Cheeks, which had a red Colour, but such a tawny one, as that of blasted Goosberries. This Gentlewoman was then in Town with *Marinda*'s Mother, who was her Aunt, and she was an excellent help to her Cousin, both diverting her from Melancholly with her Company, and helping her with her Advice: When *Celadon* came to Lodge there, he became acquainted with her; and having remembered, that he once had some discourse with her, while the Prince was entertaining her Cousin, he call'd to mind, how Witty and Pleasant he that time found her Conversation: Their being in the same House, made them often in one anothers Company, and in a little time they grew to a great Familiarity. *Celadon*, hearing what a considerable Fortune she had, made his Addresses to her in earnest, but found her still grow strange, when he spoke to her of that, and therefore thought that something extraordinary was the cause of it: in the mean time the Prince grew reconciled to *Celadon*, and as their falling out, was only a pretence for *Celadon*'s leaving him to Lodge there, so the Prince now made use of that priviledge to his own advantage; for now *Marinda* could no longer avoid him; and though she did as often as she could, yet he came so often thither, that sometimes he lighted on her before she was aware: *Celadon*'s Chamber was on the same floor with hers, and nothing but a small Gallery divided them;

her Chamber was just at the Stair-head, and the Prince would sometimes, as he came up Stairs, find her Door open, and then force himself into her Company: He this way had frequent access to her, yet could never gain from her the least word in his Favour.

In this posture his Amour was, when an Express* came to him, that the King had set out of *Dublin*,* on his March to *Limerick*; the Prince gave the Officers notice to have all the Souldiers in Arms the next day to receive him: He went streight to see *Marinda*, because he did not know but the King might take him along with him, as he came through the Town, and so not give him time to take his leave of her: He came into her Mother's, and being used to go often thither to *Celadon*, went up Stairs, without speaking to any body; not seeing her below, he went into her Room, but not finding here there, and seeing her Closet-door open, and a Pen and Ink on the Table, he pulled the Door close, and sat down to write a *Billet Doux*,* which he intended to leave for her: In the mean while *Marinda* came into the Room, and this Cousin with her, and sitting down, they carried on a discourse, the first words of which the Prince did not hear, but the following were to this purpose: 'I tell you, *Marinda*, (*said the Stranger*) 'tis in a happy hour for you, that the King is coming down, for he will take these Souldiers with him, and this Prince, who is so ungentile to endeavour the ruin of a Gentlewoman': 'I should scarce blame him (*said* Marinda) for why should a Man be blamed for prosecuting the way to his own happiness? Nor am I so conceited, as to aim at Marriage; for what private Gentle-woman could nourish such vain hopes as those, of being raised to a Princess? 'Tis more than a bare Prodigy, for Earthquakes, Inundations, and those wonders of Nature do sometimes happen; but that a Prince should marry a private Maid, is such a wonder, as I never found mentioned in all the Chronicles I have read'. 'What? Cousin, (*says she*) and do you plead for him! will you ever consent to his Love on dishonourable terms?' 'No, (*said* Marinda) as I do his Cause Justice, so I will my own;

had not this news of the King's coming prevented me, I would have gone with you to your Father's, to avoid him; now I will deferr it till I hear the Siege of *Limerick* is over, then I will retire to your House, or some other Relations, where he shall never trouble me again, or I him'. 'Ay, do, *Marinda, (said her Cousin)* fly the Tempter: But what shall I do with my Lovers? They are both going to the Camp, and will expect that I give them some satisfactory answer; and I do not know which way to incline; the one is a Captain of Horse, he is approved of by my Father, but disliked by my Mother and me, because he is a Papist,* and I have another cause of aversion for him, that is, that he is a Foreigner; I don't fear that all his Country Jealousie can make him suspitious of such a Face as mine; but those on the continent make such saucy domineering Husbands, that no free-born *Irish*-woman* will endure their slavery: There is *Celadon* a good Humoured, Handsome, Witty Fellow, and one that I like very well; he makes his Courtship so zealously, and swears so seriously that he Loves me, that I do almost believe him; yet the Fellow is so poor, that I fancy neither Father nor Mother will ever consent to my having him; prithee tell me what resolution to take; or whether of the two to favour, my inclination, or my Obedience'. 'There is (*said* Marinda) come to this Town an *Indian*, who tells Fortunes very true': 'Shall we (*said she*) put on our Masks, and go to her?' 'No, (*said* Marinda) she will come to me for sending for; I was the first that received her in this Town, and wellcom'd her as a Stranger, and therefore she is very intimate with me': 'Then pray (*said the Stranger*) let us send for her immediately': ''Tis not a fit time (*said* Marinda) but in the Afternoon I will send her a Message by my Maid, and she shall bring her with her; but we are summoned, here's a Servant come to call us to Dinner'. They went down together, and the Prince stole softly to *Celadon's* Room, and finding him within, bade him come along with him to his Lodgings; and he bearing the Prince company out, no body suspected, but he had all the while been in *Celadon's* Chamber.

As the Prince walked towards his Lodging, he told *Celadon* of his lying hid in the Closet, and all that he over-heard them saying. 'And now *Celadon*, (*said he*) what think you of my Condition?' 'What should I think, (*answered* Celadon) but that you are happy? for you love and are beloved': 'But what good will that Love do me (*reply'd he*) since 'twill never avail me any farther than the bare acknowledgment? Nay, that she Loves me is rather my unhappiness, for did she not, perhaps she would continue here, and I might have those smaller satisfactions, the sight of her, and her Conversation: And I would rather have her Company, though she tortur'd me with disdain, than lose her by this effect of her Love'. 'Your Highness (*said* Celadon) has better Politicks in War than in Love; if in the Battel your Enemy should fly, would you grieve that he did not stand longer, does not his flight do better? If she had strength enough to resist she'd stand; but she, like him, in her flight confesses her weakness, and in retiring before you does seem to say, *Come follow me, and Conquer.* Your Highness saw her Cousin, my Mistress, though her Face is very ordinary, yet her Shape is handsome; she has a very taking Wit, and I hear she has a Bag of Money would blind one sooner, than the most dazling Beauty: And (as I am a Souldier) though I have a great devoir* for all the Beauties of the fairer Sex, yet, to my thinking, rich Jewels out-shine the brightest Eyes, and the yellow of the *Leuidores** is a more glorious colour, than the fairest White and Red, that ever made Lover doat, or Poet Rhime: I am glad they will send to the *Indian*, for I'll tell them their Fortunes, and order them too, but so much to our advantage, that you shall have your Mistress, and I mine; the way I will go about it shall be this: Your Highness may desire your Landladies pretty Niece to take her Maid with her, and go to the *Indian* to know her Fortune, let her order the Maid in the mean time to stay at the Door, and when the Servant comes from *Marinda*, let her pretend to be the *Indian*'s Servant, and to carry the message up Stairs; let her bring the Servant down word, that her Mistress, the *Indian*, is busie with Company, but will wait upon her Lady in the Evening; then let the young Gentlewoman gratify the *Indian* well for telling her Fortune, and tell her that she has a mind to have a Frollick that Night, and desire the *Indian* to lend her one of her *Spanish* Suits to Masquerade in: When she has brought this Suit home, I will put it on, and go to *Marinda*'s at the appointed time; I will personate the *Indian*, my feigned Voice is shrill enough to pass for a Womans, you know I have got a Foreign tone, as well as she, my height and shape are much the same, and for my Face 'tis no matter, she always wears a Veil, so will I, and as to her gift of Fortune-telling, let me alone to tickle their Fancies'. The Prince was mightily pleas'd with the Stratagem, and said, '*Go on and prosper, thou cunning* Proteus,* *and may* Celadon *the Prophetess have better luck than* Celadon *the* Franciscan'.

The Prince sent up for the young Gentlewoman, and telling her that there was an *Indian* come to Town, who shewed none but Gentry their Fortunes, he desired her to go this Afternoon to ask hers; and told her, that she must borrow a *Spanish* Suit of the *Indian*, as for her self: He gave her a Purse of Gold to pay the expence, and leave as a pawn for the Cloaths, in case the *Indian*, not knowing her, should be unwilling to venture them without Security. The young Gentlewoman took her Maid with her, and did her business as successfully as they could wish: She had her Fortune told, and the Prince, to whom formerly she made the whole Relation of her Amour, was desirous to know what the event of it would be. She told him, that the *Indian*, smiling, delivered it in these words; *Be Constant, and be Happy.* *Thank your kind Fortune, Madam,* (said the Prince) *how many a Lover would be over-joy'd at such a Prediction!* He spake this with a particular earnestness: The Fair Virgin gave the Prince thanks, for sending her to know it, and took her leave of him, not without observing something extraordinary in his Countenance, by which she guess'd that the impartial God of Love, has no more respect for Persons of Quality, than for their Inferiours. *Celadon* fell to shifting himself, and having put on the *Indian*'s Habit, looked so like her, that the Prince promised himself both Diversion and Success from this adventure. *Celadon* staid till it grew duskish, because the Night would help the disguise; about an hour after he came back again, and gave the Prince this account of his Success.

'I have been at *Marinda*'s, she took me into the Closet (where you was) very cautiously, lest any one should hear but her Cousin and me, not dreaming who she confessed her self to: She told me that she did Love you, and yet must dissemble it; that she heard your Highness had been in the House, and she thought 'twas to see her; that she expected you would come to take your leave of her, and did not know how she ought to receive you: She said that I told her at first, that she should have you, but now desired me to confess freely, whether I spoke truth then, or did it to flatter her humour; for if it were so, she would not indulge her self the sight of you any more, but wean her self from you for altogether. I found by this, that the *Indian* had soothed her up with the hopes of your Marrying her; I humoured her too, and bade her hope the best: For had I done contrary, that would have contradicted what the *Indian* told her, and given her some grounds to suspect me for a Cheat; besides, despair might have made her refrain your Company for ever: She sighed, and said, she would ask my Advice, whenever she had occasion for it. Then her pert Cousin took me up, telling me much the same story that you over-heard her in, and desired to know which of these Lovers she should have: Your Highness may imagine I gave the Verdict on my own side: And after threatning her with all the ill fortune, that can be in the other Servant, I promised her as much happiness in my self; and was so large in my own praises, that it made me blush, under my Veil, while I uttered them. She proffered me a reward for what Advice I gave her, yet would not tell me whether she would take it or no.

But when I had parted with them, and thought the Joke was over, the pleasantest part of it was to come; for at the Door I met a pretty young Lady, who was come to pay a visit to *Marinda*: I was at the Ball (*says she*) when you professed the faculty you have, in fore-telling Events, and now I have met you in a private House, I must needs make tryal of it; saying this, she took me aside, and having conjured me Secresie, she told me, that she lived in *Dublin*, and was ardently sollicited by one *K—k,** a great Officer in the Army; that he made her vast promises of kindness and everlasting Affection; and she desired to know whether he would prove Constant, if she trusted him: After having looked fixedly on her Face, and the palms of her Hands, and used those impertinent Formalities, that your pretended Fortune-tellers do, I bade her never doubt it, my Life for it he would prove true. She could not conceal the Joy she conceived, at my favourable answer; and for my good news, and to bribe me to Secrecy, she clapp'd a *Jacobus** into my Hand. I hope your Highness will not blame me, for cozening* the poor Maid, for I thought it might prove my own case another time, to desire one to have the same good Opinion of me, and therefore I thought I ought to do, as I would be done by. In the Street I was stopped again, by a spruce Servant Maid, who making a low Curtesie or two, desired me to look in her Hand, and give her a proof of my Skill; she brought me into a Kitchen, to a light, and shewed me her Hand, but begg'd me to be secret, because it concerned her Reputation: I told her, she might speak freely to one who knew not her Name, nor was ever likely to see her again. I am Courted (*said she*) by an Old Man, who is very Rich; I love a Young one,* who is very poor: The Young one I dare not marry, for fear of Beggery; the Old one I must not, because I cannot endure him: In this uncertainty I would live as I am, were it not that the young Man took his advantage on me in the Critical minute; and now I must make choice of one, or the other, for fear of being with Child, and for ever disgraced; tell me, in this case, which will thrive best with me.

I remember'd I was *Celadon* still, for all my Habit, and therefore considering the necessities of those Youths, whose niggardly Fortune would not let them Marry, and the Dotage of feeble old Age, that will needs be Lovers, when their season's past, I advised her to Marry the Old Man, and keep the Young one; that way (*said I*) you will enjoy the Love of the one, and the Riches of the other. Her Master coming in at that time, and asking what I was, the Maid told him, I was a Fortune-teller: Go thy ways, Girl, (*said he*) and leave me to speak a word to her: When she was gone, he pulled out a Silver Groat,* telling me, I should have that to resolve him a question. Sir, (*said I*) though I sometimes tell the Poor their Fortunes for nothing, yet I never do it to the Rich under half a piece. I am not one of your ignorant rambling Gypsies; I'll tell you your Fortune, as it shall fall out to a Hair: Well, here's half a Piece for you, (*said he*) if you tell it so exactly, for 'tis a thing of moment: I am about to marry a handsome Girl; the only scruple I have against it, is, that these young Jigglets* are so wild, that I fear 'twill be hard to keep her constant; tell me therefore, whether she will be true to me, or no? What Age are you of, (*said I*)? But threescore and eight, (*said he*): I looked in his Hand, and took his Gold, and told him, that the Virgin would prove as honest to him after Marriage, as she was to her Vertue, before he Weds her. This was a true answer, for I fancied it was his own Maid that he meant, and how honest she was, I knew by her own Confession. I went away laughing at the folly of Covetous old Age, that would throw more Money away, towards the satisfying an impotent desire, than he would willingly have given a Physician, for the saving his Life'.

The Prince laugh'd at the pleasant use which *Celadon* had made of his disguise; and they two debated for a while which was the greater weakness, that of the Old Man, to trust his Honour to a Young Woman's Vertue; or that of the Maiden, to trust hers to the Constancy of an Officer. The Prince placed his own Folly in the first rank; and said, it was greater than the other two, to trust all the repose and quiet of his Life, to the rigour of a disdainful Woman; to cringe to one that was beneath him, and submit himself to one, who could not pretend to a higher Match, than one of his Dependants: But when Love took her part, it made him recant all these Reflections, clad the meanness of his passion in a lovelier dress, and made it seem, either no fault at all, or one of the least, the most pardonable of his Life. He commended *Celadon*'s discretion, in indulging her the hopes of Marrying him, for fear her Vertue should otherwise have made her shun him.

The next morning word was brought to the Prince, that the King was near the Town: He drew up all his Men, in order to receive his Majesty; and after having kissed his Hand, and discoursed with him, concerning the preparations requisite to the Siege, the Prince came home to put all things in readiness for his next days March: But that which he accounted the chief, was to take his leave of *Marinda*. He found her alone in her Room; and though she seemed uneasie, yet he constrained her to stay, and hear a long story of his Passion; which he set forth in the most prevailing words, accompanied with the most winning Carriage, that Art and Nature, joyned together, could invent. At last he gain'd so much upon her, as that she consented to receive a Letter from him, while he was in the Camp. He came back to *Celadon* with a mixture of Gladness and Sorrow; Gladness at the favour she had granted him, the priviledge of Writing to her; and Sorrow to think that he must purchase that satisfaction at so dear a rate, as the loss of her Company, as long as the Siege should continue. I will not set down how many of these Fits of Joy and Grief he had, whilst he was in the Camp; neither will I Romance so much, as to write down all the thoughts he had of her, and all the many wise Dialogues he had with himself about her; those the Reader can better imagine, than the Author tell; at least, if he has any of the same Passion the Prince was possessed with: That will make him sympathize exactly with his Highness's thoughts, as two Clocks, well made, keep time with one another. Thus much I know, that they were so importunate with him, that they could neither be lull'd asleep, by the stillness of the Night, nor diverted by the terrors of the Day: They kept him company continually, followed him even into the Enemies Trenches, and when Shot of all sorts flew thickest about his Ears, they were neither still'd by the noise of the greater, nor frighten'd away by the small. Among all these thoughts, he did not forget those of writing to her; nor had he been three Weeks away, when calling to him one of his trustiest Servants, he ordered him to take Horse for *Clonmell*, and, with all the privacy imaginable, deliver her this Letter.

To the most Charming
MARINDA.

*I*F *I could think that Absence* would have the same effect on you, it has on me, I should be but too happy: Might I hope that it has lessened your Disdain, as much as it has encreased my Love, I should be over paid for all the restless hours, and melancholly thoughts it has cost me. But this is too good Fortune for me to flatter my self with; nor is it likely, that she who shuns her present Lover, should cherish his memory when absent. We have block'd your Enemies up, won a Fort from them, and daily gain more ground:* And O that I were as certain of Conquering you; as of taking the Town! But you, my lovely stubborn Enemy, hold out against all my endeavours: All the Assaults I make serve but to shew your Obstinacy, and my Weakness, and help to confirm the improbability of my gaining you. Yet Despair it self shall not make me give over; but like a resolute General, who will rather dye in the Trenches, than rise from before the Town which he has once laid Siege to; so after all your Repulses, my worst of Fortune shall but make me dye at her Feet, whose Heart I could never gain entrance to. But do not rashly resolve on my Ruin, but consider, my Lovely Princess, whether it is not juster for your Pity to indulge that Passion, which your Disdain cannot destroy: And so instead of proving the death of your Lover, give him his Life, in letting him live to be*

Yours,

S——g.

The Prince awaited the return of his Messenger with a great deal of Impatiency: The next Evening, as he came from an

Assault, his Man came to him; and having told his Highness that he had performed his Message to *Marinda*, he gave the Prince a Letter from her, which he opened, after kissing the Seal, and, with a great deal of Pleasure, read these words.

To the Prince of *S——g*.

*W*HEN *I received the Honour of a Letter from your Highness, I was in a great strait, whether to return an Answer to it or no: If I did, I thought it would look like Presumption; if not, like Incivility: In this hard choice I thought it best to err on the kinder side, and rather incurr the censure of Rudeness, than that of Ingratitude. How little I am guilty of the latter, your Highness, too well knows, by being witness to a discourse, which I never design'd for your Ears; but since it came to them, I cannot recant it. And though your Highness talks of despairing to take the Town, I can't think you should, when you know how much you have gain'd of it already: But your Highness deals harder with this, than you do with* Limerick; *you'll offer no Conditions, because you expect it will surrender upon Discretion; you hope that in vain: for though a Traitor within takes your part, and all the cunning you have assaults it from without, yet these ways will not render your Highness Master of this Fort, which will never yield, but upon Honourable Terms.*

Your Highness's

Most humble Servant,

Marinda.

The meaning of this Letter was too plain, to have any false Constructions made upon it; and the Prince, who saw that he must retire, or engage too far, had now a greater conflict with his thoughts, than he had before with the Coyness of his Mistress, he was so equally divided betwixt Love and Interest, that they governed his Breast by turns, sometimes one having the better, and sometimes the other. He thought, however, that so kind a Letter as this seemed to require an answer; and therefore, upon the Army's taking the *Irish-Town*,* supposing that a little more time would render the King Master of *Limerick*, he wrote her this answer, to prepare him a kind Reception, when the Camp should break up.

TO THE
Most Charming *Marinda*.

*A*s our taking the Irish-Town *has prepared our way towards the taking of* Limerick, *so I hope the Surrendry of* Limerick *will prepare mine, towards the taking that which I value above all the Cities of the Universe, my Lovely* Marinda; *and my hopes will be mightily cross'd, if one Month does not put me in possession both of that, and her: She shall then see how much better conditions we'll give her, than we do to our Enemies; when we shall make them accept of what Terms the Conquerour pleases to impose; but my Beautious Fortress, even when she has Surrender'd, shall chuse her own Conditions, and impose what Laws she pleases on her Conquerour: Since, as he receives that Title only from her Favours, so will he any time exchange it, for that of the*

Humblest of her Servants,

S———g.

In this Letter, the Prince spake what he truly thought, that *Limerick* would soon be taken;* for the King had sent for some heavy Cannon to the Camp, to throw down the walls, and a breach once made, there were thousands of *English* bold enough to have dared all the Enemies Shot, and force their way into the Town, in spite of all the resistance: But Fortune had otherwise ordered it, for *Sarsfeild** with an unusual Bravery, marched with a small Body of Horse, farther into that part of the Country which was Subjected to the *English* Power, than they suspected he durst; surprized the Convoy, and cutting them to pieces, burnt them, their Carriages and Provisions, (which they brought for the Army) to ashes; some of the Carriages he nailed up, and burst the rest; and the Army wanting them to batter the walls, and the hasty approach of the Winter, not giving them time to send for others, they raised the Siege; his Majesty went for *England*; his Forces retired to their winter Quarters, and our Prince to his Mistress.

I trust, the Reader will not think it prejudicial to our Prince's Honour, to come back without taking the Town, this was not his fault, but his Fortunes; the days of Errantry are past,* nor have our Warriours now, such Swords as those Knights of old, that could hew a way through the thickest walls, and do wonders greater than our Age will believe: Our Prince did not pretend to impossible Exploits, but as far as pure Natural Force and Courage could go; he might have been ranked in the first File of the Army; he was not ashamed, that he could not do impossibilities, but came back to *Clonmell* with as brisk a Look, and as glad a Heart, as if he had Routed *Sarsfeild*, and laid *Limerick* in Ashes. The place where he Lodg'd before, was made ready for him, but he had other designs, and therefore Complemented some of the other Officers with those Quarters, and chose *Marinda*'s Mothers for his. But when he first accosted his long absent Mistress, 'twas in Terms so passionate, that the inability of the Author makes him forbear to express them; nor could he match them, though he borrowed *Apollo*'s Brain to invent,* and a Quill plucked from one of Cupid's Wings to write them down; neither would he think it safe to express them to the Life if he could, lest a Passion so well represented might prove infectious to those that Read it; and such Charming Words like those in Magical Books, might raise a Spirit in some Fair Reader's Mind, some rampant Spirit, that would make the Raiser his prey, before she would be able to lay him again: Thus much the Author will assure you, that they had as powerful an effect, as he could desire over his Mistress; or as the most Amorous of my Readers could wish to have over his own: She laid aside that reservedness which she observed to other Men, and confessed her Love, as freely as she gave it him; that Night, he told *Celadon* of the welcome he received; and *Celadon* asked him, whether he intended to

Marry her? This Question put the Prince to a stand, and he asked *Celadon* whether there was any possibility of Enjoying her without it: *Celadon* told his Highness, he would try, and acquainted him with the way, and the Prince approving of it, the next afternoon he put it in Execution: He went to wait on *Marinda*'s Cousin, whom he Courted, and they two being pretty Familiar, the young Gentlewoman began to talk about the Love the Prince bare her Cousin; she did it to sound him, and to find whether the Prince's Affection was real. *Celadon*, who watched for such an opportunity, said, yes truly, the Prince had an unfeigned Affection for her fair Cousin, so violent a one, that notwithstanding the difference of Quality, the Prince would Marry her if he were single. 'What, is he Married then', said the young Lady, extreamly surpriz'd? 'Why, did not you know it, Madam', *said he?* 'since through inadvertency I have blabb'd it out, for Heaven's sake do not let it be known that it came from me, for then I shall be for ever out of the Prince's favour'. She promised she would not, and so left him, to carry the News of it with all speed to her Cousin.

The Prince having left a great part of his Men in *Clonmell*, was gone out of Town* that Morning at the Head of the rest, accompanying the gross of the Army which was Marching towards *Dublin*; and on the morrow about mid-day, he took leave of the Officers, to return to *Clonmell*; he brought but one Man back to wait on him, who had a Horseman's usual Arms, Sword and Pistols, and the Prince had a slight Morion on, and a Buff-coat, both which he wore, rather for the solemnity sake, (because he went with the Army) than for any use he suspected he should have of them: Riding along, they came to diversity of Roads; where he and his Man being both Strangers to the Country, lost their way, nor could they meet with any one to direct them into it, only the Voice of some body in a wood just before them; when they drew nearer, they heard the shrieks as of one in distress,* and the Prince Riding up, overtook his Man, and put on as hard as he could to see what it meaned; coming nigh, he saw by a Hedge side two Men, who had defended a gap against twelve, one of them was fallen, and block'd up that place in his Death, which he maintained whilst alive; but was not unrevenged, for two were killed on the other side, and the other Person stood armed with Anger and Despair, and with more Courage than Hopes, maintained the Combat against so unequal a number; the single Person seemed by his Garb to be a Gentleman, he had only a half-pike, which he managed so actively, that with it, he kept off a row of pitch-forks and Swords, which assaulted him; behind him, stood a Lady and her Maid, crying out at every thrust they made at him, and calling upon Heaven and Earth for assistance, against those barbarous Enemies.

The Prince rode up, and commanded them to desist, and let him know what was the cause of their Quarrel; one of them gave him a short Answer in *Irish*, and at the same time made a thrust at him with his Pitch-fork, which by the Prince's sudden spurring his Horse missed him, and ran the Beast into the belly, the Prince drawing out a Pistol, returned the *Irishman*'s Complement with a shot, and laid him dead at his Horse's feet; he had done the same service with his other Pistol, but that the Beast enraged with the double wound which *Teague*'s weapon* had given him, kick'd and flung so, that the Prince was forced to alight; the Man which waited on his Highness, did more Execution with his Pistols, and having with them, killed one, and wounded another, he alighted and drew his Sword to Fight by his Master, who by this time had dispatch'd two more, not without receiving a great wound, which one of them with a half-pike had given him in the side; the Prince enrag'd at that, fell fiercer on the rest, and the Stranger who hitherto had been only on the defencive part, having but one to deal with, gave him his *mittimus** to the other World, and came up to fall on those who had more than their hands-full of the Prince and his Man; but at his coming, finding themselves too weak, they sought that safety in their heels, which their Swords could not give them; the Prince and his Man had Jackboots on, and were unable to follow them; and the Stranger was so weary with the

Blood he had lost, and the weariness of so tedious* a conflict, that he had scarce strength enough to keep him on his Legs; however, he used that little he had in coming up to the Prince, and thanking him for his own Life, and his beautious Companions; the Prince told him, he owed it to his own Valour, and the favour of Heaven, which seldom fails to help the Couragious, especially when they have Justice on their side.

The Prince ordering his Man to look to the strangers Wounds and bind them up, went himself to Compliment the Lady upon her delivery: He found her leaning on her Maid, bewailing the Death of that Stranger who was killed before he came there, but how was he amazed, when looking in her Face he found it to be *Marinda*: When he first came in to her assistance, her Hoods were over her Face; which was the Reason he did not know her, and the Beavor of his Morion* being down was the cause of the like ignorance in her; though he very little expected to meet her there, yet the joy to see her safe, overcame his amazement, and he was about to testifie it, with all the extasie which his Passion raised in him: When she, casting an angry frown at him, said, 'I thought, Sir, to have given my Deliverer the greatest thanks for the rescuing yonder Gentleman's Life, and my Honour, from the Hands of these wicked Villains; but since it is to you I must pay them; I must at the same time declare, that I had rather they should have taken my Life, than, forced me to owe it to you; go, leave me to be a prey to them whom thou hast hunted away, for I had rather dye here, bemoaning this poor Gentleman who fell in the defence of my Honour, than take refuge with you, who whilst you defend it from others, endeavour to prey upon it your self'.

He answered her very mildly, and would fain have expostulated with her concerning his Innocence, but she sat over the Dead Gentleman bewailing him, and would not hearken, nor answer one word to what he said; the Prince having found her so kind at his last seeing her in *Clonmell*, wondered strangely at this Capricio of his Fortune, and turning away from her, went to the wounded Gentleman, to see whether he could unfold

him the Riddle. He said, all that he knew of it, was, that the
Dead Gentleman was a professed Servant to her, as he was to her
Cousin, and that *Marinda* having made a sudden resolution to go
for *Dublin*, they two proffer'd to accompany her thither; that she
would not let them take as much as a Man with them, because
she would not have any one know which way they were gone;
that she had desir'd them to avoid the High-roads as much as
they could, because she had no mind to be known by any who
came from *Dublin*-ward; that in this by-road they met those
Rapperees,*who bade them deliver; that the Gentleman who
Courted her, shot at one of them and killed him; that then they
all fell upon them two, who had no other way to defend
themselves and the two Women, than by letting them go
behind them, and they defend that gap, till some others Riding
that Road might come to their help; that the Gentleman was
killed, as he made a pass at that second Man who lay Dead by
him, and that himself, snatching up the Dead Man's half-pike, as
being a better defence than his Sword, had held them all in play
till he came into his Rescue. The Ladies expressing so great a
resentment against him, made the Stranger curious to know who
it was; but the Servant had no sooner informed him that it was
the Prince of S——g, but he begged a thousand pardons for the
rudeness his ignorance made him commit; and said, that his
Highness had acted with a Bravery suitable to his Quality; and
that though he never before had the Honour to know him, yet
what he had seen his Highness perform in this little
acquaintance, should make him respect him more for his
Deserts, than his Title. The Prince had very little relish for all
the Praises the Stranger heaped upon him, and only desired him
to prevail with the Lady, to go back to *Clonmell* with him.

    While the Prince's Man went to catch the Horses, the
Stranger persuaded *Marinda* to return back with him; and getting
all upon the Horses, they rode before, only the Prince got upon
his Man's, and the Man on the Dead Gentleman's, and laying
the Body before him, they Rode to the next Town; the
Gentleman's wounds were slight ones, and needed little Cure,

besides rest and a recruit of Blood; therefore he went with *Marinda* the next day to *Clonmell*; but the Prince's wound was large, and had lost him so much Blood, that his Life was in danger. *Marinda* the next day sent him a Surgeon, and a Hearse, to carry the Gentleman to *Clonmell*, he was Buried there, and she shewed such an excessive Grief at his Funeral, that no one who knew he Courted her, but thought that she Loved him; the Prince's being wounded came to *Celadon*'s Ears, but he wondered that it was in rescuing *Marinda*, whom he thought all the while to have been at home; he streight took Horse and came to the Prince, and found him very weak, wanting rest, and incapable of taking any: To hear that his Rival was so bemoaned by *Marinda*, was worse than Poyson to his wounds; to have seen her prefer another before his face; one who was Dead, and insensible of her Kindnesses, before him, who valued them at so high a rate; and to think, that the other, who was but a private Gentleman, was preferr'd by his Mistress, before him and all his Titles, raised a Noble Indignation in him, which bespread his Face with a redder dye, than that of his Wound. When he had told *Celadon* her unkind Behaviour towards him; he guessed immediately what was the Reason of it, but would not tell the Prince, for fear it should incense him: He only made a slight matter of it, and told his Highness that if he would write a Line by him, for a pretence to him to see her, he would soon accommodate the difference; and set him as much in her Favour as ever; the Prince seemed to give but little credit to these hopes, but because he would leave nothing unattempted, ordering that no body should disturb their privacy, he bade *Celadon* write, whilst he dictated him these words.

TO THE

Incensed *Marinda*.

*I*F it be a Fault to have rescued my Fair One from her Enemies; if it be a Crime unpardonable, to have spent a great part of my Blood in

revenging the death of my Rival, because I did not lay down my Life
with his, then will I offer up the poor remainder of my Blood, to atone
for the Cowardise I have been Guilty of; and shall think my Life sold
at too dear a rate, if it should draw so many precious Tears from your
Eyes, as did that happy Gentleman, who even in his Death triumphed
over the Love of his Survivor. But if I was as willing to expose my self
for your sake, and he was the first in your Defence, only by the good
Fortune, of being with you at the beginning of the danger; I know not
why the living Servant should not share more of your favour than the
dead one; since he would have died as willingly at your Feet, had not
your Fortune commanded him to live till he conquered your Enemies.
Now he has kept his Life too long, since it is become odious to you,
and would gladly lay it down before the Face of his incensed Divinity,
if his weakness would permit him to come there: And if he has any
desire at all to live, it is only so long till you let him know in what he
has offended you: This sure is the least you can grant to one, who was
once so happy in your favour; and 'tis all the satisfaction your
Criminal desires, to know why you have condemned him, since he has
always been the

Faithfullest of your Servants,

S——g.

When *Celadon* got to Town, he came streight to *Marinda*'s: She
was not to be spoken with, but he met with *Diana*,* (so was his
Mistress called) and after the usual Complements past, he asked
her how he should speak with her Cousin: 'No way, (*said she*)
there's no access for you, because you come from the Prince'.
'Why, Madam, *said he*, is not *Marinda* satisfied that the Prince
has sufficiently hazarded his Life in her defence, but that she'll
endanger it farther by her Cruelty?' 'Cruelty! (*answered she*) why
what kindness can he expect from a Virtuous Woman? Or
what would the Wedded *S——g* with the Chaste *Marinda*?'
'And is that all the reason of her Anger? (*said* Celadon), Has the
poor Prince suffered all this for a word of mine? By Heaven
(*Madam*) the Prince is single, and I am perswaded has as vertuous designs on your Cousin, as I have on you'. 'If he has no

more on her (*answered she*) than I have on you, he would never again be at the expence of a sigh for her: For your part, I here discharge you my acquaintance; your mischievous Jest has been the cause of a great deal of Grief, both to my Cousin and me, for the Gentleman's death, the other Gentleman's weakness, and the endangering the Prince's Life: You have jested fairly, you had like to have jested the Prince at once out of his Life and Mistress, your-self you have jested out of my Favour, I will assure you; and so farewell good jesting, Mr. *Celadon*, for if I ever any more admit of your Jests, I'll give you leave to make a Jest of me as long as you live'.

Saying this she flung away into her Cousins Room, and all that *Celadon* could say, could not get either of them to speak a word to him. She told *Marinda* that the Prince was innocent, and, by *Celadon*'s Confession, had no designs, but what were honourable and virtuous: At the same time the Maid came up, and brought them a Letter, which *Celadon* sent to *Marinda*, and the same which he had written from the Prince's Mouth; the Servant told them that he was returning to the Prince, and desired to see them before he went, that he might know what Service they had to command him. Neither of them would consent to see one who had been the Author of their late troubles: But *Diana* told her Cousin that the Prince, who was innocent, ought not to suffer for him; that she should rather shew her self kinder than ever, to one she had so causelesly tormented: *Marinda*'s own Love did take his part so much, and joyn so prevalently with her Cousin's Arguments, that it made her give some small interval to her Griefs, to pay that which was due to her Love. She wrote a Letter, and sent it to *Celadon*, who made what haste he could to leave an angry Mistress, to see his wounded Prince, and cure his Body, by this sovereign Ballsom* which he brought for his mind. The Prince (when he came before him) would not stay to tell him how he did, till he first asked how he had succeeded. *As well for you, Sir,* (said he) *as you can wish, and as ill for my self; how ill for my self, I will tell you hereafter; how well for your Highness, this Letter will acquaint* *you.* At these words he gave him the Letter; and the Prince, with a great deal of haste, breaking it open, found these words.

To the Prince of S——g.

*H*OW shall I be silent, when Justice obliges me to confess I have *wronged you? Or how shall I have the face to confess a Rudeness, which a misunderstanding made me guilty of? I was too rash to condemn you without a hearing; but I hope your Highness will pardon that rashness, when you shall consider it was in the defence of (that which I prefer before all things) my Vertue. Though the weakness of my Sex makes me careful of my life; yet did your Highness need it, I could willingly expose it as lavishly in your behalf, as you did yours in mine: Yet my Innocence (which is dearer to me than that Life) I must not sacrifice, no, not to you. Your Highness has more Generosity, than to begrudge a Gentleman a few Tears, who lost his Life in my defence: They were no more than what I owed both to Gratitude and Humanity: Neither ought you to infer from thence, that the Dead shares more of my Favour than the Living: I would convince you of the contrary, if it were fitting: But your Highness's condescention must not make me forget, that you are a Prince, and that my highest desires rise no higher than to be the*

Humblest of your Servants,

Marinda.

'You deserve all things, Divine *Marinda,* (*said the passionate Prince*) what Title is too High, or Estate too Magnificent to admit you for a Partner? I will no more indulge this vain Ambition, or let it cross my Love: Tell me, *Celadon,* (*said he*) does not *Marinda,* with her natural Beauty look finer than our Proudest Court Ladies, tho' decked with all their Gaudy Costly Dresses? Yet that lovely Body is but the Shell of a more glorious Inhabitant, and is as far out-shone by that more radiant Gust,* which lies within, as your choicest Jewels exceed the lustre of the Cask, which holds them: For her Illustrious mind

has got as inexhaustible a store of rare perfections in it, as the
famed *Potosi** has of Riches: And as in that the greedy *Spanish*
Conquerour, the farther he diggs, finds still more new supplies
of Ore; so whoever makes himself Master of her richer Heart,
will still discover there new Mines of Radiant Vertues, so infi-
nite they are, that they would tire the most inquisitive Lover to
find them all, and each of them has such peculiar Charms in't,
enough to make him leave his scrutiny after more, to admire
that one which his first search does find'. 'Ah, Sir, (*said*
Celadon,) now your Highness is happy and in favour, you do
not consider him who is clearly cast off by his Mistress, for
what he did only with design to serve you; for it was my telling
Diana that your Highness was married, and confessing the fals-
hood afterward, has so put me out of her favour, that she has
forbidden me ever seeing her again'. 'Tho' (*said the Prince*) that
was an unlucky Policy of yours, yet since 'twas well designed,
you shall not suffer for it, and therefore take my word, that the
same day which makes me happy, shall make you so to; and as
our Loves are joyn'd, so shall our Fortunes'. 'Your Highness
(*said* Celadon) cannot be more in Love with the perfections of
your Mistress, than I can with the Wit and good Humour of
mine: Besides, her Baggs which are so large and tempting, it
would grieve my heart to part with them, after I was in so fair
a way for obtaining her'. The Prince answered, that both their
Loves waited only for his Health, and then he would soon see
them consumated. He wrote two or three Letters more to
Marinda whilst he lay ill, but the Reader must excuse me, if I
produce them not here, since *Marinda* burned them to prevent
a discovery; and Secretary *Celadon* was not so careful to keep
any Copies.

Now had the active Sun run through our Celestial sign,
and his pale Sister gone through her Monthly course, and
changed her Orb, whilst the poor Prince kept his Bed, and
with the loss of Blood had been as pale as she; at length the
help of Art restored his Health, strengthning Nature began to
exert her power, and tho' she was not risen of a sudden to her

former vigour, yet she made great advances, and every day per-
ceived her strength encreasing: His impatient Love would stay
no longer than till he was able to travel, and then it carried him
back to *Clonmell*, to see his long absent Mistress: He rode to his
Lodgings at *Marinda*'s Mothers, but hearing Musick in the
House, and the Mirth of Company within, he asked what was
the Matter. "Tis, (*said one*) a preparation for Madam *Diana*'s
Wedding, who is just now to be Married'. 'Married! *said*
Celadon, O that I had either come sooner or later; for my
Honour sake I cannot see my Mistress Married away before my
Face, and yet I am come too late to prevent it; but what can be
done on such a sudden I'll do'. Saying this, he alighted, and
rushed into the House, and the Prince followed him in to see
what his design was. *Celadon* entered just as the Ceremony
began, and with a threatning voice cryed, *I forbid the Banes;**
and if the intended Bridegroom will defer his hopes so long, to go aside
with me, I will convince him, that my Title to her is better than his.
The Company wonder'd to see this Challenge laid to her; her
Relations, who were by, expected her to speak; but she was
prevented by the Bridgeroom, who fiercely cryed, that it
belonged to none but him, to vindicate his Title to her: Some
Officers were there, the Bridgerooms Friends, and would have
taken up his quarrel, but forbore out of respect to the Prince,
expecting what he would do in it.

The Prince knowing the Gentleman to be the same whom
he had seen Combat with so many Enemies, to save *Marinda*,
had such an opinion of his Valour, that he would fain have
decided the Quarrel, without injuring either of the Pretenders:
Had she been at his disposal, *Celadon* should have had her, if at
her Parents, they had decided it for the *Spaniard*: Therefore he
thought it best to leave it to her self, and therefore spoke to this
purpose. *Gentlemen, I have such an esteem for you both, that I*
would not have you fight, since, which ever falls, the Law will lay hold
on the other, and so in striving which shall have the Lady, both of you
will lose her; if you will stand to my advice, let it be thus. Refer your
Cause to the Lady, and give her three days time to consider of it, in

which time let both of you have free access to make your Court to her, and at the three days end, let her take which she will: If, Celadon, *her choice does decide it against you, you must submit; but if she like you best, there is no reason why your staying with me in my illness, should make you lose your Mistress.* The Gentleman said, that, since he owed his Life to the Prince's Valour, he would not deny him this; and *Celadon* was glad to win so much to try his Fortune in.

While the three days lasted, the two Suiters took their turns to Court *Diana*: On the fourth day, the Musick play'd again, the Priest was present, and the admiring Company stood in suspence, to see who was the destined Bridegroom. The Bride stood out, and in making her Choice, spake thus: *You are here come together, my Relations, and good Acquaintance, to see me Married, and I am happy in having the choice of two Gentleman, the refused of which may, if his deserts are answered, have many a better proffer; however, if they were ever so good, one of them must be rejected, therefore I would not have the disappointed one take it ill that I refuse him. One of them has been longer my Servant, but the other was more zealous while he was so: The* Spaniard *has been the more Complaisant, but the* Englishman *the Fonder: The* Spaniard *the truer Courtier, but the* Englishman *the truer Lover; therefore, as commonly Love is soonest raised in one Breast, by seeing it first in the other, so the* Englishman *has the advantage of the* Spaniard, *and my heart catched that Passion, as it were by Contagion from his: Yet, on the other side, I should not forget my Duty; my Father takes the* Spaniard's *part, well, but Love takes the* Englishman's: *Then I must beg my Father's pardon, if I leave the* Spaniard *to receive his reward from him whom he courted, and desire the Company to judge, if I ought not rather to yield him my Love, who sued to me for it, than to him who Courted my Parents.*

The Company was divided in their opinions, as their Acquaintance byassed* them; and some murmured at the Inconstancy of her Humour, whilst others applauded her Choice. *Celadon* ran to give her thanks, with all the kindest expressions his Joy could inspire him with; and his Rival, distracted with Grief and Shame at his unexpected repulse, stood uncertain on that sudden Emergency, how to behave himself: He was awaked out of this Trance, by a Gentlewoman, who came to him, and said, 'Take heart, Seignior, be not ashamed of a Denial, which not your want of Merit, but my Contrivance was the occasion of; 'twas I that persuaded the Lady to refuse you, and I trust you will pardon me, when I say it was for my own sake that I did it'. Without question the Company thought this an odd sort of Confidence, for a Gentlewoman to Court a Man, in so kind terms, and so pub-lickly too: Her Garb was very fine, her Shape and Air gentile, and her Face, which was one of the most amiable ones there, spake her to be in the prime of her years; yet neither her Dress, Youth, Beauty, or Love, could prevail the least on our discon-tented *Spaniard*, who would not once vouchsafe to look on her. 'What then, (*said she*) is my Constancy thus requited? Or can two years time cause so much alteration, as to make *Astolfo* forget me?' These words made the *Spaniard* turn towards her, and he no sooner saw her Face, but he cry'd out, 'Am I in a Dream? Or do I truly behold once again, the Face of my beloved *Faniaca*? Now, *Celadon*, I yield thee up thy Mistress, and quit all my pretensions to her, for this which I have newly found'. *Celadon* gladly thanked him for his submission to *Diana*'s Choice, and all the Company bore a part with the *Spaniard* in the Joy he conceived at the change of his Mistress: But the beautiful *Indian*, who longed to hear how he came for *Ireland*, said, 'It is now, my *Astolfo*, two years since you and I parted, wonder not then if I am desirous to know what befell you since that, and how you escaped a Death which so appar-ently threatned you; my endeavours to find you out here, made me relate all the passages of our Acquaintance hitherto, and therefore I believe there is no accident in the remaining part of your Life, which is too secret for the Ears of this hon-ourable Company'.

'I have had none, (*said he*) which I will not freely tell, but to the understanding my Relation, it is requisite that this Illustrious

Company should know some things, which for want of opportunity, have as yet been a secret to you, as well as to them. My Father is a Gentleman of a plentiful Estate near *Sevill*, by my Mothers death he was left a Widdower with two Children, Me and a Daughter, both which he was very fond of, as being his only Comforts, the Relicts of his deceased Wife, and the Pledges of his youthful Love: There lived near us an old Couple who had the like number of Children, a Son and a Daughter, they were intimate Friends of my Father's, and so free with us, that notwithstanding the severe restraints of our Countrey upon young Persons, yet our Families observed no such Custom, but we young ones conversed with one another with the same freedom as if we had been near Relations: And as youthful familiarity in different Sexes, usually ends in Love, so it proved with us, for our Neighbour's Son and my Sister had such a mutual Affection, that they were never well but in one anothers Company; and his Sister, whether by her own inclination, or their setting on, seemed as uneasie unless when she was in mine; had she been handsome, perhaps I should have taken as much diversion in his Sister's Company, as he did in mine; but I thought those Complements thrown away, which were bestowed on an ugly Face; nor could my Wit help me with one fond Vow or happy Expression, for want of Beauty to inspire it; This made me avoid her Company to get into his; but when I saw him shun mine as much, and that he and my Sister coveted to be always together; his growing more reserved to me than formerly, and some symptoms which I perceived in my Sister; her frequent sighs at parting, her blushes at meeting him, and some other slips, which the most dissembling of your Sex find difficult to hide, gave me apparent cause to think that she loved him. He and I were once as great as 2 *Brothers,* laid our Breasts open to one another, thence his never discovering the least to me, concerning his passion for my Sister, made his Love look to me, as if it designed nothing that was honest.

I had then to wait on me a *Turkish* Captive, who was taken away young, and having been bred up several years in my

Father's House, was very trusty and discreet; I let no one know
my suspitions, but him, and ordered him to be a Spy on all my
Sister's Actions; and if ever he observed any thing remarkable
between them two, that he would acquaint me with it: He
observed my Commands, and one time brought me word, that
he had over-heard him and my Sister discoursing; that she
desired him to ask her of my Father, and that very soon, or she
should be discovered to be with Child, and so be disgraced,
and turned out of Doors; tho' this was but what I feared to find
out, yet now I found those fears true, it enraged me both
against him and my Sister: However, the consideration of her
Sex's weakness (which is an unequal Combatant for Love,
when assisted by earnestness and opportunity) made me pardon
her so far, as to leave her to be punished by the ill conse-
quences of her own Folly; but him I resolved to be revenged
on: Tho' my blood boyled at the first sight of him, yet I dis-
sembled my anger in publick, and told him that I had something to impart to him, if he would take a walk with me into
the Fields in the cool of the Evening; he consented, and we
went out together; as we walked on talking, I drew him insen-
sibly to a private place, and then retiring a little distance from
him, I bade him draw: Sure you are in jest (*said he*) you will
not draw that Sword against your Friend, which you have
before now drawn in my defence: This Sword (*said I*) was
drawn then for my Friend, but now against the worst of mine
Enemies, one who has abused my Friendship, and my Sister's
Love: Yet thus much I will give to our former Affection,
Marry her, and salve up the Injury thou hast done her, and I
will forgive thee mine: What, (*said he*) and are you turned a
Bravo to hector me into Marriage? Know then that I will never
do it, neither shall it ever be said, that *Guzman** valued his
Honour so little, as to make a Wife of his Whore. Whore! (*said
I*) that word I will engrave on thy traiterous Heart; at these
words he leapt back and drew, I made at him with a great deal
of Fury; but being appeased by some Blood I drew from him,
I proffered him again the same conditions of Reconciliation;

but his Rage made him deaf to Reason: We fought on, till one thrust I made at his Breast ended our difference, by his fall.

I fled in all haste to the Sea-side, where by good chance there was a Ship under Sail bound for the *Indies*; I went aboard her; Landed in *America* amongst some Souldiers, who were sent to re-inforce our Country Garrisons there: I was a private Souldier, till a Fight that I signalized my self in, raised me to a Captain's Commission; 'twas in this station I was, when I came acquainted with you: You know the Captain of the Man of War, which boarded us, sent me Prisoner to *Sevill*, with my other Countrymen: Near this Town my Father lived; I sent him word of my being in Prison, and he streight came to see me, but told me, he must not own me for his Son, lest it should cost me my Life: He applauded my revenging the dis-honour done to my Family; but said, that there had been Warrants issued out against me, and 500 Duckats, by the deceased's Friends, promised him that should seize me; that if I should stand a Tryal, and escape the Law, yet their private revenge would reach me; therefore, he said he would make Friends for me and my fellow Prisoners, that we should be dis-missed, and then he would have me spend some years abroad, and when Time, or Death had cured the malice of my *Enemies*, he would get my pardon, and call me home. I took his advice, and as soon as I was freed, hearing that the *Hollanders* were rais-ing Souldiers,* for some design they had not yet divulged, I entered Volunteer into that Party which came for *England*; you have all heard how we succeeded, and that instead of a Battel, we came as it were to a Triumph; for the *English* came over to our side;* thence we took Shipping for *Ireland*, and in *Dublin* I received a supply from my Father, which bought me the Command of a Troop; I was at the *Boyn* near *Schomberg** when he was killed; I lay in the Camp before *Limerick*, and took my chance of War, among those Brave Men that fell in the Trenches; I Quarrelled with the Prince t'other Night, mistak-ing him for some Rival that Serenaded *Diana*; but the Guards coming up, and my finding out my Errour, delivered me from his Sword too: I was afterwards engaged with ten *Irish* at once, and fortunately rescued by the Prince's Valour; so that my kind Stars preserved me through all these dangers, to fall the second time a Victim to your Eyes, my former Conquerours; I Courted I confess that Lady, but it was, because I saw not the least likelihood, of ever finding my Beloved *Faniaca*; and therefore, I thought her Fortune would prove a good shelter for a Banished Man, who had been tossed from *Spain* to the *Indies*, from the *Indies* to *Spain*, from *Spain* to *England*, from *England* hither, and one, that durst not set foot again on his Native Country: Besides her Wit and good Humour, placed her much in my Esteem, though all those Perfections vanish in any Woman, when you my incomparable Mistress are by'.

Thus the *Spaniard* ended his Relation, and the Company with no little pleasure, reflected on the alterations of Fortune; which, after tossing them so far asunder, by the contrary gusts of Adversity, now by one prosperous Gale, brought them together to their desired Harbour: The two Happy Couple, would willingly have prevented all future dangers, by fastning that indissoluble Knot, which nothing but Death can untye, but *Marinda* desired her Cousin, to forbear hers for two or three days; and the Fair *Indian* desired her *Spaniard*, to defer their Joys so long, it not being fit, that she should be admitted to so Solemn a Ceremony of the Church,* as that of Matrimony, till she were first listed among the number of her Children: The Priest who came there to Celebrate their Marriage, performed this Solemnity, and all the Company wished the Fair Convert Joy: Mirth and Feasting took up the rest of the day, and made up an intire Friendship, between the Brisk *Celadon*, and the Valiant *Spaniard*, who now Quarrelled no longer for a Mistress.

But if some good natured Reader should be too much concerned for the Amorous Prince, whose Intrigue seems to have stood still, whilst the others have run almost to the end of their Race; let him know, that his went the same pace with theirs; though the Author, to comply with *Marinda*'s Modesty, brought her not so openly acting the Lover's part, as he did the brisk *Diana*, or the bolder *Indian*; for as the main wheel of a Clock, though it turns all the rest, yet goes it self with such an insensible motion, that to an unskilful Eye it seems to stand still; so the Prince's and *Marinda*'s Amour, was carried on indiscernably to others, and seem'd to them to be at a stand, whilst indeed it was the chief mover of the two other Intrigues, and pointed out to them the long wished for, the Matrimonial Hour: You must therefore understand, that after all the dark unsuccessful days which our Prince had sighed away, in doubtful Hopes, distracting Fears, and his last black ones of Despair; Fortune vindicated her old Title of Inconstancy, in being kind to him again, in bringing him that propitious critical minute, in which they say, the Coyest Lady (if you nick the right time) is to be won:* The Prince exactly hit it in the first Visit he made *Marinda*; as soon as the designed Marriage was deferred, and the Company gone, he went to pay his particular Respects to the Lady of his Vows: He found her in the Garden with her Cousin, discoursing about the unexpected breaking off her Marriage, and *Celadon* according to his priviledge, taking her into an Ally aside, left the Prince in another, with *Marinda*; and what time they had there together, he improved to the utmost, in shewing her how sincerely he had been her Servant, from the first sight he ever had of her, till then; and told her, what he required of her in retaliation, and upon what Honourable Conditions he expected it; she answered with all the kindness due to so fond a Lover, and with a mixture of that submissive Civility, which she paid him as he was a Prince, tho' one who professed himself her Servant; and that his Highness might not censure her to have been either Rude or Cruel in her Behaviour towards him, through the whole course of their Acquaintance; she desired, that he would hear those things from her Cousin's Mouth, which she thought not so fit for her own; *Diana* was called for, and *Marinda* desiring her to acquaint the Prince with all she knew of her Thoughts, without disguising any thing;

she Discoursed with *Celadon* apart, while her Cousin began thus to the Prince, who was more than ordinarily attentive.

'When my Cousin ordered me to tell you her greatest privacies, those of her Love; she did but give the Reins to that passion, which has alwaies been too strong for her, since first the Graces your Highness is master of, reduced her to the condition of a Lover; and I question not, but she has had undeniable proofs of an equal Affection in you; or else, (by what I know of her Humour) she would rather have Died, than once suffered it to be known; your Highness over-hearing our Discourse at the Well, opened a light to the discovery of that Affection, which otherwise had been doom'd to perpetual obscurity; for though your Highness, did make some Addresses to her, which as she told me, served to ruin her the more, yet they would never have proved any advantage to you; since we both thought, that you spoke out of Raillery more than any serious design; besides, in the highest tide of her Passion, she professed, she would rather suffer any thing than own it to you; the first Night your Highness Serenaded her, she shewed so little concern at it, till you were gone, that I thought it had been a Frolick of the *Spaniard*'s Gallantry, who about that time came acquainted with me, 'twas I spoke to you out of the window, though when the difference of Voice discovered my mistake, I broke off the parly; that time the *Indian* came to Town, and lighting first into my Cousin's Acquaintance, she told her the Dream she had about you; I will not tell it over again, because your Highness has heard it already, only in vindication of the *Indian*'s Skill, let me assure your Highness, that she told my Cousin, she should have the Gentleman she Dreamed of; she interpreted the little Archer, who was on your side, to be Love, the Giant on hers, Honour; that Honour's going over to your side, and leaving her defenceless, signified, that your proffering to Marry her, would overcome her obstinacy; and the Cupid's shooting her through, is easie enough to be left to your Highness's Explanation; the *Indian* promising her success, made her indulge that Love, which she bridled before, and brought her abroad to the Ball'.

'*Marinda*, Madam, was not at the last Ball', *said the Prince*: 'Yes, Sir, *said* Diana, if your Highness remembers, there were two in *Spanish* Dress, the one was the *Indian*, the other *Marinda*'; 'But sure, *said the Prince, Marinda* was not with her in my Room the next day'.

'She was with your Highness both times, *said* Diana; nay, it was she whose Advice you asked in the Closet; she came home that Night, with all the marks of a violent Grief, at something which your Highness had said to her, and resolved withall, never to see, hear, or speak to you more; when she represented the Fortune-Teller, she forbad your Highness to prosecute the Intrigue any farther, unless you designed to carry it on Honourably; and your going on with it, by giving her your Company so often afterwards, and the *Indians* still averring that she was destined for you, made her believe, your Highness had altered your mind for the better; as you know, Lovers above all People are aptest to believe things will come to pass fortunately, meerly because they would have it so; this her belief was strengthned by the kind promising Letter you sent her from *Limerick*; which Letter, induced me too, to think that your Highness had designed something to her advantage: You saw what a free reception she gave you, at your return from the Camp, till *Celadon*'s telling me that you were Married, dashed all the Joy I conceived at the prosperity of her Amour, and was very near breaking her Heart, in endeavouring to gain a Conquest over her Love; but when she found how difficult that was, she said, she would punish your illegal Passion, and her own at the same time; and lest a fit of Love should make her recant, she put it in Execution immediately; there was a Gentleman of a considerable Fortune, who had seen her at my Father's in *Dublin*, and fallen in Love with her; this Gentleman being then come to *Clonmell* to see her, she desired him to wait on her to *Dublin*, and I desired my Servant the *Spaniard*, that he would accompany her thither; she told me, that she would rather Marry him whom she did not Love, than give a longer encouragement to any unlawful Affection, which your Highness might entertain for her; that would have bereaved you of her for ever, had not she been met by those Rapperees; her Servant fell there, and though she was mightily concerned for your Highness's danger, yet her Vertue drew those Tears from her, which she thought due to her Defender's Misfortune; and might serve to make you despair, ever coming into her favour again: But when *Celadon* undeceived us, by telling me that your being Married, was only an invention of his own, Shame and Love returned very powerfully upon her; Shame, that she had used you so ill without a cause; and that Love, which before was only supprest by her Resentments, flourished now with greater vigour than before; This discovery which regained your Highness her Affection, lost *Celadon* mine; and my Anger at his crafty deceit, and his being the cause of so much bloodshed, (though innocently) made me resolve on the same way to get rid of him, which my Cousin designed against you, that is, by Marrying another; and the *Spanish* Gentleman, who had my Father's Consent, coming then wounded from a Journey which he undertook to serve me; I thought once to reward his Service, and punish *Celadon*'s Falseness, and imagined I might do it with less disturbance, whilst your indisposition kept him out of the way; but Fate, which they say presides over our Marriages, as well as our Deaths, ordered it otherwise, and brought him just time enough to suspend it'.

The Prince gave the most ample demonstrations of Joy, at the setledness which this Relation shew'd to be in *Marinda*'s Love; and having thank'd the Ingenious *Diana* for the comfort she had given him, he walked towards the other Couple; they joyned Company, and the Prince desired *Marinda* that she would compleat his Happiness, by setting *Celadon* as high in his Mistress's Favour, as himself was in hers: The Beautiful *Marinda* granted him this request, as the first demonstration of her Obedience; she endeavoured it so effectually, that presently she made her Cousin pardon *Celadon*'s former miscarriage, and receive him again into her favour; neither did *Marinda* find it any thing difficult to persuade her to this; for of all People, Mistresses are the most forgiving, indulgent Persons to those they Love; and let them dissemble it as much as they please, they cannot be long Angry at any fault a Lover commits, unless it seem to proceed from want of Affection; but *Celadon* not being of that Nature, was soon forgiven, and as a proof of it, was encouraged to hope she would Vote for him: The next morning, the *Indian* came to wait on the two Cousins, and told *Diana*, that he who was in Election to be her Husband, was the *Spaniard* whom she had been so long looking for; *Marinda* had invited her to the Wedding, and she came in a little after the Prince had deferr'd it, and then seeing it put off, would not discover her self to the *Spaniard*; she desired *Diana* to keep him still in ignorance, that when he was refused, she might see how he would excuse himself to her: *Diana* desired no less than she, that it might be kept secret, lest *Celadon* should esteem her love the less, thinking that the *Spaniard* being owned by another, made her take him for a shift; this was the result of the three days Tryal, and hence it came to pass, that the *Spaniard* dejected at the loss of one Mistress, was elevated by the unexpected finding out another, whom he Loved better.

The short prorogation of their Marriages, only continued till the Prince had prepared for his; at last the expected day came, and rewarded the three longing Lovers with the intire possession of their Mistresses: The Beautiful *Marinda*, the Ingenious *Diana*, and the Pritty *Faniaca*, submitted themselves to the power of their Youthful Conquerours. *Diana* had all the felicity she could wish, in having him she Loved; the *Indian* gained not only her dear *Spaniard*, but a Fortune with him, for he that day received News from his Father, that his old Enemy was Dead, his Pardon taken out, and with it, he had orders to come home, and take possession of an Estate his Father gave him; the Beautiful *Marinda* received the reward of her invincible Vertue, in Loving and being Beloved, and in having gained a Prince, who raised her Quality as high (in comparison of what she was before) as a Woman's Ambition could desire; these were the Pleasures of the Wedding Day, heightned by the addition of Musick, Feasting, and Mirth; but the Night came, we must like their Bride Maids, conduct them to their Beds, and drawing the Curtains leave them there, to the full Enjoyment of those Pleasures, whose Raptures, none but Experienced Lovers know, and the Constant ones may expect to attain.

FINIS.

Notes

title-page *Vertue Rewarded; or, the Irish Princess*: The title 'Virtue Rewarded' echoes, or contests, elements of Stoic philosophy, especially the writings of the Roman philosopher Seneca (*c*.4 BC-65). Seneca, who is alluded to elsewhere in the novel, makes virtue its own reward: see 'I must Live Thus with my Friend, Thus with my Fellow-Citizen, Thus with my Companion. And why? Because 'tis just; not for Design, or Reward: For it is Virtue it Self, and nothing Else, that pleases us', *Seneca's Morals abstracted: In three parts: I. Of Benefits II. Of a Happy Life, Anger, and Clemency III. A Miscellany of Epistles*. By Roger L'Estrange. III, Ep. XIII, 'Every Man is the Artificer of his Own Fortune. Of *Justice, and Injustice*' (London, 1679), p. 101. See also below, note to p. 106 'Be Constant and be Happy'.

Vertue Rewarded; or, The Irish Princess is one of the earliest fictions to include reference to Ireland in its title. In particular, its conjunction of 'virtue' with an 'Irish princess' makes a strong contrast with the recently-published anonymous fictions, *The Wild-Irish Captain, or Villany display'd truly and faithfully related* (London, 1692), or *The Irish Rogue; or, the comical history of Teague O Divelley, from his birth to the present year, 1690* (London [1690]). The name Teague O Divelley derives from a play *The Witches of Lancashire and Tegue O Divelly, the Irish-priest* (1682; 1691) by Thomas Shadwell (1642–92).

title-page *She ne'er saw Courts ... Gond. lib. 2. Canto 7*: The first two books of the unfinished heroic poem *Gondibert* by Sir William Davenant (1608–68) were published in 1651. The quotation, accurately transcribed, is the sixth stanza of Book II, Canto VII. In the light of 'The Story of Faniaca' (see pp 72 ff), it may be noted that among Davenant's other works was a theatrical entertainment, *The Cruelty of the Spaniards in Peru* (1658).

title-page: *Richard Bentley* (bapt. 1645–1697) was chiefly known for publishing prose fiction, leading his fellow stationer, John Dunton, to dub him 'Novel Bentley'. He included *Vertue Rewarded* in his twelve-volume collection of *Modern Novels* (1692–93), the only work to bear the date 1693 on its title-page.

p. 35 *Marinda*: Despite the use of type-names elsewhere in the novel (see below nn. to Celadon and Astolfo, pp 42 and 77), Marinda was not a common name in seventeenth-century literature. Between 1625 and 1693, it occurs only in Thomas Betterton's low comedy, *The Revenge* (1680), and as the name of a Spanish woman who retained her chastity under threat of rape by

keeping raw beef under her armpits until it rotted, as related in the anonymous *The Glory of God's Revenge against the detestable sins of murder and adultery*
(1685); the name was subsequently used by Sir Richard Blackmore for that of
a very minor character in the heroic poem, *Prince Arthur* (1695). See also
Appendix, pp 156–9.

p. 35 *Innocent Country Virgin*: In a seventeenth-century Irish context, the praise
of rural innocence over the deceits of the court is more than novelistic cliché,
alluding rather to the tendency of the contemporary Protestant settler community to portray itself in just such terms, especially in contrast to the metropolitan centre represented by England.

p. 35 *Fucus*: 'Paint or cosmetic for beautifying the skin; a wash or colouring for
the face' (*OED*: 'fucus' 1).

p. 37 *The Dutchess of Suffolk*: Katherine Brandon (née Willoughby; Bertie by
second marriage), duchess of Suffolk (1519–80). In 1533, at the age of 14,
Katherine became the fourth wife of Charles Brandon, duke of Suffolk; a
Protestant, she left England during the reign of the Catholic Mary Tudor.
The anecdote is garbled, however, for the bishop in question was not
Edmund Bonner (see below, n. to p. 37, 'the Bloody Bonner') but the bishop
of Winchester, Stephen Gardiner (*c*.1495x8–1555). The story is told in John
Foxe's *Acts and Monuments* (1563; 9th ed. 1684), also known as the '*Book of
Martyrs*': 'Another time my Lord her Husband having invited me and divers
Ladies to Dinner, desired every Lady to choose him whom she loved best,
and so place themselves: My Lady your wife taking me by the hand, for that
my Lord would not have her to take himself, sayd that for so much as she
could not sit down with my Lord whom she loved best, she had chosen him
whom she loved worst' (*Acts and Monuments*, 3 vols [London, 1684], III, p.
779). Foxe described Gardiner, who was imprisoned in the Tower of London
and deprived of his see under the Protestant Edward VI, only to be freed and
restored following the accession of Queen Mary, as 'a man hated of God and
all good men' (II, p. 447).

p. 37 *the Bloody* Bonner: Edmund Bonner (*d.* 1569), bishop of London between
1540 and 1549, when he was deprived of his see under Edward VI; he was
reappointed to the bishopric by Queen Mary in 1553 and again deprived of it in
1559 after Mary's death. Bonner gained the epithet 'Bloody' for his zeal in
pursuing and condemning heretics, over 100 of whom were burned at the stake
in his diocese during the reign of Queen Mary; a late-seventeenth century work
described him as 'that Blood-thirsty Monster, and *Cannibal* of the Age' ([Anon.],
The History of the Life, Bloody Reign, and Death of Queen Mary (London, 1682), p.
34.

p. 37 *sate*: i.e. sat.

p. 37 *the main Story is true*: Many contemporary prose fictions opened with an
assertion that the story about to be told was 'true', as with the full title of
Aphra Behn's *Oroonoko, or, The Royal Slave: A True History* (1688). It is now

accepted that Behn did indeed visit Surinam, where much of the action is set, and her work incorporates mention of individuals whose presence there is historically verifiable, but no source for the principal narrative of Oroonoko is known; see, for example, J.A. Ramsaran, 'Oroonoko: A Study of the Factual Elements', *Notes & Queries* 1960, 7 (4), 142–145; Bernard Dhuicq, 'Further Evidence on Aphra Behn's Stay in Surinam', *Notes & Queries*, 1979, 26 (6), 524–6; Angeline Goreau, *Reconstructing Aphra: A Social Biography of Aphra Behn* (Oxford: Oxford University Press, 1980), pp 43–69; Dhuicq, 'New Evidence on Aphra Behn's Stay in Surinam', *Notes & Queries*, 1995 42 (1), 40–41; and Janet Todd, *The Secret Life of Aphra Behn* (London: Andre Deutsch, 1996), pp 38–42. The situation is similar in the case of the (much fuller) historical material to be found in *Vertue Rewarded*, and the narrative concerning the principal characters. For an influential discussion of the connection between 'the deep and fruitful analogy between questions of truth and questions of virtue', see Michael McKeon, *The Origins of the English Novel 1600–1740* (Baltimore and London: Johns Hopkins University Press, 1987), esp. parts I and II (p. 22).

p. 37 *Liberty of Conscience*: The Westminster Confession of Faith (1646) defined liberty of conscience as freedom 'from the doctrines and commandments of men which are, in any thing contrary to his Word; or beside it in matters of faith or worship' (XX, ii, 'Of Christian Liberty, and liberty of conscience').

p. 39 *that mighty River*: The Nile.

p. 39 *trace it to its Spring*: The (still-disputed) source of the Nile had been a matter of scientific interest since classical times; in the seventeenth century the Jesuit Pedro Páez (1564–1622) traced the source of the Blue Nile to Lake Tana; his account, unpublished until the twentieth century, was however used by many seventeenth-century writers, including Athanasius Kircher, *Mundus Subterraneus* (1664–78) and Johann Michael Wansleben (or Vansleb), *The Present State of Egypt* (1678).

p. 39 *Zudder Sea ... Diques*: The Zuider Zee is a large inlet of the North Sea, situated in the north-west of Holland; though dykes maintain its stability, it has been subject to very serious flooding over the centuries, with considerable loss of life.

p. 39 *drowzy* Hollander: The slowness of the Dutch was proverbial.

p. 39 *Philosopher's Stone*: A legendary substance believed capable of turning base metals into gold; belief in it had still not entirely disappeared in the late-seventeenth century.

p. 40 *our present King*: King William III (1650–1702) who, with his wife Mary, was joint ruler of England, Scotland and Ireland; following Mary's death in 1694, William became sole monarch.

p. 40 *battle at the* Boyn: The decisive battle between the Protestant forces of Prince William of Orange (William III) and the Catholic army of James II, fought near Drogheda on 1 July 1690 OS (12 July 1690 NS).

p. 40 *Limerick*: After its defeat at the Boyne, the Jacobite army withdrew to the west of Ireland, occupying the stronghold of Limerick, the site of two major sieges in 1690 and 1691.

p. 40 *three Kingdoms*: i.e. England, Scotland and Ireland.

p. 40 *Forreign Troops*: William III's army included not only English, Scottish and Irish Protestant troops but Danish, Dutch, German and French Huguenot soldiers.

p. 40 *Prince of S———g*: The use of the name *S———g* in the present context immediately brings to mind Frederick Herman, duke of Schomberg (1615–1690), William III's commander-in-chief; he, however, was killed at the Battle of the Boyne (see below, n. to p. 129). The commander of the forces that entered Clonmel in the third week of July 1690 was his third son, Count Meinhard Schomberg (1641–1719), who had commanded the right wing of William's army at the Boyne; created duke of Leinster in 1691 he became third duke of Schomberg two years later. The details of the relationship between *S———g* and Marinda, culminating in marriage, have no apparent correspondence to historical fact, making the implied identification puzzling.

If the Prince of *S———g* is an intentionally composite figure, then it is worth noting that the commander of the Danish mercenary troops who fought for William of Orange in Ireland, following the treaty negotiated by Robert Molesworth (1656–1725) was the German duke of Würtemberg-Neustadt, known to contemporary writers as the 'prince of Wirtemberg'; see, for instance, James Shirley, *The True Impartial History and Wars in Ireland* (London, 1692), p. 133.

p. 40 *Clonmell*: Clonmel (*Cluain Meala*) in Co. Tipperary stands on the River Suir. In the seventeenth century, Clonmel was a walled town, famous as the site of Oliver Cromwell's greatest military defeat in Ireland on 17 May 1650, when the besieging New Model Army of some 8000 men was repulsed by a 2000-strong garrison commanded by Hugh Dubh O'Neill; Cromwell lost more than a quarter of his troops in a single day. It was originally expected that the forces of James II would defend the town which a contemporary work described as 'Naturally Fortyfied, standing on an Advantagious ground, very hard to be Attackt; besides, it's Invironed with a very good Wall and Castle of great strength', *An Account of the Nature, Situation, Natural Strength, and Antient, and Modern Fortifications, of the Several Cities and Garrison-Towns in Ireland; that are still possessed by the Forces of the Late King James …With the Several Approaches by which they may be Attack't. By an Irish Officer, who served in the Army under the Late Duke of Ormond* (London, 1690), p. 7.

p. 41 *great Battel*: The author may have had in mind the battle at Baile Urlaidhe (now the Barn Demesne) between the victorious Déise and the routed Osraige; accounts of the battle are to be found in the eighth-century saga, *Toirche na nDéise* (*Expulsion of the Déise*), and in *Foras Feasa ar Éirinn* by the seventeenth-century writer, Seathrún Céitinn, or Geoffrey Keating (*c.*1580–before 1644).

p. 41 *Crown of* Mounster ... *Inhabitants*: Ireland was originally divided into five provinces or *cúigí* (fifths): with Míde (Meath) in addition to the four modern provinces of Leinster, Munster, Connacht, and Ulster. This division of Ireland did not long survive the eleventh-century Norman invasions and the fact that the author of *Vertue Rewarded* knew of the *cúigí* suggests a certain degree of familiarity with Irish history, a possible source being Edmund Campion's *Historie of Ireland* in *The Historie of Ireland, collected by three learned authors viz. Meredith Hanmer Doctor in Divinitie: Edmund Campion sometime Fellow of St John's College in Oxford: and Edmund Spenser Esq* (Dublin, 1633), p. 1; the works are separately paginated.

p. 41 *Chief Street*: Clonmel was unusual among seventeenth-century Irish towns in having a High Street (now O'Connell Street), suggesting the author's knowledge of the town; see also below, n. to p. 48 'High-street'.

p. 41 *Enemies of their Liberty and Religion*: Williamites hailed their cause as a triumph for political liberty over absolutism and arbitrary power and for the Protestant (especially Anglican) faith.

p. 42 *hard Quilt*: A simple bed or unpadded mattress made of rough fabric.

p. 42 *Celadon*: Céladon is the hero of Honoré d'Urfé's pastoral novel, *L'Astrée* (1607–27).

p. 42 *King's coming to the Town*: See below, n. to p. 103, 'the King had set out of Dublin'.

p. 43 *Younger Brother of a good Family*: Military service was one of the few acceptable choices of career for younger sons of the aristocracy and gentry.

p. 44 *Dorick Order*: Doric is one of the three principal orders of classical architecture, along with the Ionic and Corinthian.

p. 44 *the Great* Moracho: 'Moracho' appears to be an attempt at a phonetic rendering of an Irish-language name, where 'Murchadha' (modern Irish Ó Murchú) would seem the most appropriate. Hubert McDermott suggested the original might have been William Morroghow, listed in 1661 as one of the 'old burghers' of Clonmel; see *Vertue Rewarded; or, The Irish Princess*, ed. Hubert McDermott (Gerrards Cross: Colin Smythe, 1992), p. ix. This identification is highly unlikely, however, since Morroghow was a dispossessed burgher banished to Connacht in the wake of the Cromwellian conquest and refused permission to re-enter the town in 1661; see W.P. Burke, *History of Clonmel* (Waterford: N. Harvey & Co., 1907), p. 96. A more likely original would be Richard Moore, a glover from Barnstaple in Devon, who took up residence in Clonmel in 1655, becoming a wealthy land-broker and, by 1685, a great sheep farmer (Burke, pp 91, 102). It was Richard Moore who entertained the Lord Lieutenant of Ireland, the earl of Clarendon, during the latter's visit to Clonmel in the early autumn of 1686; see P. Melvin, 'Sir Paul Rycaut's memoranda and letters from Ireland, 1686–1687', *Analecta Hibernica*, 27 (1972), p. 133, quoting BL Lansdown MS1153, vol. I.

p. 44 *mighty* Scythian ... *Terror of the World*: Tamerlane or Timur (1336–1405), son of a shepherd, was the greatest central Asian military commander since Genghis Khan (*c.*1162–1227). In Christopher Marlowe's *Tamburlaine the Great*, the warrior exhorts his sons to follow his example with the words 'When I am old, and cannot manage arms/Be thou the scourge and terror of the world' (*Tamburlaine the Great,* Part II, Act I, Scene iii). The author seems to misremember the play, however, for none of his sons is the equal of Tamburlaine himself.

p. 44 *Alexander the Great*: Also known as Alexander III of Macedon (356–323 BC), one of the greatest military commanders of all time. The reference to the 'Rich Man of the East' is obscure, since the description does not fit well either with Alexander's regent, Antipater, or his steward Demophoon.

p. 44 *Arcadia*: A region of Greece on the Peloponnesian peninsula, Arcady had long been celebrated for its pastoral culture in the Golden Age; the Italian literary Academy of Arcadia was founded in Rome in 1690.

p. 44 *Meen*: i.e. mien.

p. 45 *Small-pox*: Smallpox was a common infection throughout Europe in the seventeenth century (and would remain so until vaccination against it became widespread in the nineteenth century); as a result, an unscarred or lightly scarred face was accounted a feature of beauty among contemporaries.

p. 45 *Carnation*: A 'light rosy pink' (*OED*, 3. A 1); used as an ideal for human flesh colour.

p. 45 *Stature*: As with her colouring, the young woman singled out by the prince is described in idealized terms familiar in much seventeenth- and eighteenth-century literature.

p. 46 *President*: i.e. precedent.

p. 47 *our dancing days are gone*: cf. Capulet's 'You and I are past our dancing days', William Shakespeare, *Romeo and Juliet*, I. 5. 31, but already proverbial; see Morris Palmer Tilley, *A Dictionary of the Proverbs in England in the Sixteenth and Seventeenth Centuries* (Ann Arbor, MN: University of Michigan Press, 1950), D118.

p. 48 *High-street*: See 'Chief Street', n. to p. 41 above.

p. 49 *Mother-in-law*: i.e. stepmother.

p. 49 *Emperour's Court*: The court of the Habsburg Holy Roman Emperor, Leopold I (1640–1658–1705).

p. 49 *in this Island*: Pejorative accounts of Ireland have a long history, from the work of Gerald of Wales, or Giraldus Cambrensis (*c.*1146–*c.*1223), through the writings of Edmund Spenser, Edmund Campion, Meredith Hanmer, and others – and were the norm in the seventeenth century in English-language literature, and never more so than at times of civil strife. Only rarely did more positive sentiments find their way into print, making the following statement about the Irish by the supposedly English writer of *The Character of an Irish-Man: or, a Dear-Joy Painted to the Life* ([London], 1689), highly unusual for the period: 'They are Civiliz'd as much as We; a Nation of as much Humanity, Temperance, and Sobriety' (p. 3).

p. 50 *Mark Anthony*: Marcus Antonius (*c*.83–30 BC), Roman general and triumvir. The reference is to Mark Antony's perceived abandonment of Rome for the sake of Cleopatra; contemporary readers of *Vertue Rewarded* would have been more familiar with the hero of John Dryden's tragedy *All for Love* (1678) than Shakespeare's *Antony and Cleopatra*.

p. 50 *Blockadoes*: i.e. blockades.

p. 50 *Count* Epithalamium: An epithalamium is a wedding song; the tune the author has in mind may have been the popular epithalamium, 'Thrice happy lovers', from *The Fairy Queene*, (1692) Act V, by Henry Purcell (1659–95).

p. 50 *Why should my fair Enchantress sleep*: Like other verses in the novel, this seems to be original to *Vertue Rewarded*.

p. 52 *Night-rail*: A loose wrap or dressing gown.

p. 52 *old Abby*: The Franciscan abbey of St Francis was built in 1269, the oldest surviving part of the building dating from the fourteenth century. It was largely destroyed at the Reformation and was in ruinous condition when Capt. John Stevens (*c*.1662–1726), soldier, translator and antiquary, visited it on 11 May 1689, when serving with the Jacobite army. Much later, Stevens described Clonmel monastery in terms that echo the description in *Vertue Rewarded*:

> The Church was one of the finest in *Ireland*, and there were several fine Tombs in it; for besides those of the Founders and Benefactors, there were those of the *Prendergasts*, the *Mandevils*, the *Brays* and the *Whites*, all of *English* Extraction; besides the stately Monument of one of the *Butlers*, Baron of *Cahir*, which was rais'd in the midst of the Choir, the usual Place for the Founders, which has made many believe they were such. That Tomb was all of Marble, with very curious Figures and Bass-Relieves ... To conclude, there was in this Church a miraculous Statue of St *Francis*, which was us'd to set before such as were to take an Oath; because it had been often found that those who durst presume to forswear themselves in its Presence, were immediately punish'd, being overtaken by some remarkable Judgment.

[John Stevens], *Monasticon Hibernicum; or, the Monastical History of Ireland* (London, 1722), pp 276–7.

p. 52 *thought her Common*: i.e. a common prostitute.

p. 52 *hall'd*: i.e. hauled.

p. 52 *Jilt*: Variously meaning a kept mistress or a common prostitute, 'jilt' was a new word in the seventeenth century, the first usage noted in *OED* dating from 1672.

p. 52 *gentilely drest*: i.e. genteelly dressed.

p. 53 *Fame, who is most commonly a great Lyar*: Proverbial; Tilley F44.

p. 53 *Harlequin*: Originally a Venetian representation of a gauche servant from

Bergamo, in Italian *commedia dell'arte*, the harlequin, known by his parti-coloured costume, had become familiar on the English stage by the late-seventeenth century.

p. 53 *touze ... hale*: Tousle, or treat a woman indecently; to pull roughly, or molest.

p. 53 *Chip in Porridge*: '[A]n addition which does neither good nor harm, a thing of no moment' (*OED*, porridge n. P2); cf. John Dryden, *Troilus and Cressida*, II, iii, 174.

p. 54 *Bravo*: A daring villain or assassin.

p. 54 *Dublin*: The Irish capital was by far the largest city in Ireland in the seven-teenth century, with a population of around 60,000, and had long been at the centre of the Pale (or 'English Pale'); accordingly, metropolitan Dubliners tended to consider even the larger English towns of provincial Ireland, such as Clonmel, to be rustic or uncouth.

p. 54 *wild* Irish: One of several pejorative terms, including 'savage Irish', 'mere Irish', or *'fior-Ghael'*, for the native, Roman Catholic (and supposedly bar-baric) Irish of predominantly Gaelic stock – or simply for those who lived beyond the Pale.

p. 55 *Beelzebub*: Identified with the Philistine god Baal (Ba'al Zebûb) or 'Lord of the Flies', Beelzebub is second to Satan among the fallen angels in Milton's *Paradise Lost* (1667; 1674), I, l. 81, but here, perhaps, simply 'the Devil'.

p. 55 *Capella*: (Latin): A she-goat.

p. 56 *incognito*: In disguise.

p. 56 *Abbey*: See above, n. to p. 52, 'old Abby'.

p. 57 *jumping*: Coinciding.

p. 57 *Spark*: Lover, suitor.

p. 58 *Out-landish Man*: A foreigner.

p. 58 *Limerick*: After his defeat at the Battle of the Boyne in July 1690 (see above, n. to p. 40), James II took ship from Kinsale bound for France. The Jacobite forces regrouped in the west of Ireland, with Limerick as their stronghold. A contemporary work described the city as 'the biggest in *Ireland*, except *Dublin* ... standing on the Banks of the *Shannon*, which encompasseth it so about that it's a perfect Island, by which means its very strong by Nature; it's also Fortified with a very high strong Wall, on which are several Bastions and Redoubts', *An Account of the Nature, Situation, Natural Strength, and Antient, and Modern Fortifications, of the Several Cities and Garrison-Towns in Ireland*, p. 3.

p. 58 *Sack*: Sherry.

p. 59 *Niobetick*: From Niobe, daughter of Tantalus, in Greek myth, who boasted of her fourteen children to Leto, leading Leto's offspring, Apollo and Artemis, to kill them all; Niobe was turned to stone.

p. 59 *Franciscan*: The Franciscan friars were founded by St Francis of Assisi (1181/2–1226) in the early-thirteenth century; under the 1697 penal legislation (9 Will III c. 1) all friars, along with other religious, were ordered to leave Ireland by 1 May 1698.

p. 59 *Plato's transmigration*: The belief that some aspect of the individual – usually the soul – survives and enters another body is generally associated with Pythagoras (mid-sixth century BC); Plato argued that souls do not remember previous bodily existences.

p. 59 *Lictor*: In ancient Rome, an officer who followed the consul or magistrate, bearing the fasces.

p. 59 *Bridewell ... Stocks ... Gibbet*: *Bridewell*: A house of correction; the original Bride Well, opened in the 1550s and intended for vagrants, was in London but the term was in widespread use in the seventeenth century; *Stocks*: An ancient punishment for petty offenders, whose feet were locked in a wooden structure in a public place, leaving them open to general ridicule; *Gibbet*: The gallows.

p. 59 *the* French: The army of James II was largely composed of French troops under French commanders.

p. 60 *Jesuitical evasion*: Equivocal or prevaricating argument, from supposed character of the Roman Catholic Jesuit order.

p. 60 *Centry*: i.e. sentry.

p. 61 *Jack of the Lanthorn*: Will-of-the wisp; ignis fatuus.

p. 62 *Spring*: The description of the spring allows for a plausible identification with a location just outside of Clonmel. Lying half a mile to the north of the town, in the foothills of the Comeragh mountains, and known at least since the mid-nineteenth century as the Ragwell, the spring is to be found in a secluded site, surrounded by a few old trees, and on an elevation from which Clonmel can be surveyed. For an early-twentieth century photograph of the spring, see http://www.rootsweb.com/~irltip2/photos/oldphotos/index.htm.

p. 62 *ancient* Irish *Chronicle*: Although the story that follows might seem plausibly to have a source in Irish chronicle or folklore, it does not appear to do so; see above, 'Introduction', pp 16–17.

p. 62 *Cluaneesha*: The name, which does not appear to exist outside the pages of *Vertue Rewarded*, is impossible for a personal name in Irish; see above 'Introduction', p. 17.

p. 62 *Macbuain*: Less problematic than Cluaneesha, this name still offers various referential possibilities. It could, variously, be an anglicization of Mac Mhumhain (son of Munster); taken from an actual 'Macbuaine', the name given by Meredith Hanmer to the first master of St Patrick, on the future saint's arrival in Ireland; or an English compositor's error for Macbrian (the name of various kings of Munster). See Meredith Hanmer, *The Chronicle of Ireland* in *The Historie of Ireland* (1633), p. 40. For the difficulties English compositors had with Irish-language names, see Ian Campbell Ross, '"One of the Principal Nations of Europe": The Representation of Ireland in Sarah Butler's *Irish Tales*', *Eighteenth-Century Fiction*, 7:1 (1994), 5 n. 10.

p. 62 *Posnanie*: Poznan, in Poland, was a place of pilgrimage in the seventeenth century but mainly among pilgrims from Lithuania, Hungary and parts of Russia. Its fame led Samuel Johnson (1649–1703) to write, in his attack on the Catholic doctrine of transubstantiation, 'Now if Christ's body in the *Pix* at Limestreet be the same individual body which is in the *Pix* at St *James*'s, or at *Posnanie* in the Higher Poland ...', *The Absolute Impossibility of Transubstantiation demonstrated* (London, 1688), pp 29–30.

p. 62 *Edith*: There are two saints by this name: St Edith of Polesworth, or Tamsworth (*c*.901–37), daughter of King Edward the Elder of England, and St Edith of Wilton (961–84), daughter of King Edward the Peaceable; both saints are associated with female monasticism, suggesting that the name was not chosen at random. However, it is also possible that 'Edith' is a version of Ita or Ite (480–570), an Irish saint with a strong cult in Munster, and again associated with monasticism, though not of royal birth (see n. to p. 62 above, 'Cluaneesha').

p. 63 *Tympany*: A swelling or tumor.

p. 64 *for the Inhabitants of* Ireland ... *Bed*: See above 'Introduction', pp 17–18.

p. 64 *Morpheus*: The Greek and Roman god of Sleep; son of Hypnos, the Greek god of sleep and dreams.

p. 64 *Yield, Soldier ... Sword*: See above, n. to p. 50.

p. 64 *Marinda*: See above n. to p. 35.

p. 66 *brave*: Here in the older sense of splendid or handsomely dressed, rather than courageous.

p. 66 *little wing'd Archer*: i.e. Cupid.

p. 68 *nice*: Delicate or refined.

p. 69 *the fall of Eve*: See Genesis 3: 1–7 (esp. 6–7).

p. 70 *observe that silence*: The desirability of women remaining silent can be traced back to Sophocles (*Ajax*, l. 293) and St Paul's injunction to women to remain silent in church (1 Cor. 14. 34), and had become proverbial by the seventeenth century.

p. 70 *abroad*: i.e. out of the house.

p. 71 *bobb'd*: i.e. tapped.

p. 71 *Sarabrand*: An alternative spelling of saraband (Fr. *Sarabande*), a slow and stately Spanish dance.

p. 72 *Faniaca*: The name has no obvious source.

p. 73 *Spartan Boy ... young Fox*: The story is told in Plutarch's 'Life of Lycurgus', given here in a translation by John Dryden: 'So seriously did the Lacaedemonian children go about their stealing, that a youth, having stolen a young fox and hid it under his coat, suffered it to tear out his very bowels with its teeth and claws and died upon the place, rather than let it be seen'; *Plutarch's Lives. Translated from the Greek by Several Hands*, 5 vols (London, 1688), I, p. 173.

p. 73 *While I am in England I should dissemble, like the English*: This curious remark echoes – perhaps unconsciously – John Calvin's rejection of dissimulation, and stands at odds with the attack on 'Jesuitical' thinking on p. 60 above.

p. 73 *Brachman*: Brahman; a member of the priestly caste of the Indian subcontinent.

p. 73 *Province of Antis*: More usually Antisuyu (*anti*[*inti*]=east; *suyu*=region), the Quechua name for the region to the east of the Inca empire (Tahuantinsuyu) in the central Andes, bordering on the Amazonian rainforest. The primary source of all the South American material in *Vertue Rewarded* is Sir Paul Rycaut's translation of the Inca Garcilaso de la Vega's *Comentarios reales de los Incas* (1609; 1617), published as *The Royal Commentaries of Peru, in two parts the first part treating of the original of their Incas or kings, of their idolatry, of their laws and government both in peace and war, of the reigns and conquests of the Incas, with many other particulars relating to their empire and policies before such time as the Spaniards invaded their countries: the second part, describing the manner by which that new world was conquered by the Spaniards ... written originally in Spanish by the Inca Garcilasso de la Vega; and rendered into English by Sir Paul Rycaut, Kt* (London, 1688); see also 'Introduction', pp 20–4 above.

p. 73 *Incas*: Incas (Inka) is properly the name for the rulers of the empire whose capital was Cuzco or a member of the royal race; often used for the whole people of Tahuantinsuyu.

p. 73 *kept up the ancient Barbarity*: cf. *Royal Commentaries*, I, v, 'Of the Government, Diet and Cloathing of the Ancient *Indians*': 'These people were as barbarous in their manner of living in their Houses and Habitations, as they were in the Worship of their Gods, and Sacrifices ... and of this sort of People there are some yet remaining ... who still continue their ancient Barbarity' (p. 8).

p. 74 *with one consent worshipped the Sun*: The Inca rulers claimed descent from the Sun (Father) and Moon (Mother), whose children Manco Capac and Mama Ocllo emerged from the waters of Lake Titicaca; the sun-god, Inti, was the single god to whom temples were dedicated. Cf. *Royal Commentaries*, I, 'The Translator to the Reader': 'they adored the Sun, whom they acknowledged for their God' (p. [iv]).

p. 74 *Tiger ... Serpent ... Amaru*: cf. *Royal Commentaries*, IV, xvii, 'Of the Idols which the *Indians* of *Antis* worshipped, and of the Conquest made over the *Charcas*': 'In those provinces of *Antis* they commonly worshipped Tygers for their Gods, and great Serpents, much thicker than a Man's Thigh, and twenty five or thirty foot in length ... called *Amaru* (p. 119).

p. 74 *Human Blood ... Captives*: Cf. Garcilaso's description of the ancient (non-Inca) American Indians in *Royal Commentaries*, I, iv, 'Of the Idolatry and Gods which the Ancient *Incas* adored, and Manner of their Sacrifices': 'The Sacrifices which they made to these Gods were as cruel and barbarous as the Gods were stupid and senseless, to whom they offered them; for besides Beasts, and Fruits, and Corn, they sacrificed Men and Women of all ages, which they had taken in the War: And some Nations of these exceeded so far in their inhumanity, that they offered not onely their Enemies, but on some occasions their very Children to these Idols. The manner of these Sacrifices were to rip open their breasts whilst they were still alive, and so tear out their Heart and Lungs, with the Bloud of which, whilst warm, they sprinkled their Idols' (p. 7).

p. 74 *Cozco*: i.e. Cuzco, the former Inca capital.

p. 74 *Madalena*: The River Magdalena rises in the Andes and flows northwards for almost 1500 km to Barranquilla, in the Caribbean. Cf. *Royal Commentaries*, VIII, xxii, 'Of the four famous Rivers, and of the Fish which is taken in those which belong to Peru': 'The first is that great River, which is now called the *Madalena*, falling into the Sea between *Cartagena*, and *Santa Maria*; the mouth of which … is eight Leagues wide' (p. 338).

p. 74 *On each side of the River there was a considerable Town*: The notable resemblance to Limerick – whose English and Irish towns were on different banks of the Shannon – and the partial correspondence between the fighting described here and the 1691 siege of the city, may not be coincidental.

p. 74 *our Canoes were made all of a piece*: cf. *Royal Commentaries*, III, xvi 'Of the many Inventions which the *Indians* made to pass Rivers, and to take Fish': 'the Invention of Boats, or such Canoes … [as] are all of one piece' (p. 81): in fact, *Royal Commentaries* notes that, unlike the natives of Florida, local American Indians did not make canoes like this, the wood of Peru being unsuitable.

p. 74 *Flat-bottoms*: The Inca use of flat-bottomed boats in warfare is described in *Royal Commentaries*, VI, xxix, p. 233.

p. 75 *Government and Religion*: The different 'Government and Religion' of the Incas is referred to on several occasions of *Royal Commentaries*.

p. 75 *Cupay*: cf. *Royal Commentaries*, II, iii: 'the *Cupay*, or Devil' (p. 29).

p. 77 *Astolfo*: In *Orlando Furioso* (1516; 1532) by Ludovico Ariosto (1474–1533), Astolfo is one of Charlemagne's paladins; the character makes his original appearance in French literature, and in earlier Italian heroic poetry, but the name was most familiar through Ariosto's work.

p. 78 *floating Bridge*: The Inca use of floating bridges in warfare is described or mentioned on several occasions in *Royal Commentaries*: e.g. III, p. 55; III, xviii, p. 84.

p. 78 *The Indian Prisoners … Nobler Captives*: Charges of cannibalism against American Indians throughout south and central America and the Caribbean were commonplace in Renaissance accounts. *Vertue Rewarded* draws heavily on Garcilaso de la Vega's description, in Rycaut's translation, of the Antisuyans; see above 'Introduction', pp 22–3.

p. 82 *Cistern*: Here, a pitcher.

p. 83 *brawny part of his Arm*: cf. *Royal Commentaries*, I, iv, p. 7; see above, 'Introduction', p. 22 and p. 23, n. 36.

p. 84 *Coca*: Cf. *Royal Commentaries*, IV, xvii: 'They worshipped also the Plant *Cuca*, or *Coca*, as the *Spaniards* call it' (p. 119).

p. 87 *Pinnace*: A small sailing vessel.

p. 87 *a few Pearl*: The wearing of pearls by Incas and other American Indians is discussed at length in *Royal Commentaries*, VIII, xxxiii, 'Of the Emeralds, Torquoises, and Pearls of that Country' (pp 341–3).

p. 88 *condemned to the Gallies*: The Spanish regularly used convicts and slaves to row galleys until the seventeenth century.

p. 88 *Sevil*: i.e. Seville.

p. 88 *Aveiro*: Aveiro lies just over 50 km north of Coimbra in Portugal, several days' voyage away; between 1580 and 1640 – i.e. the period during which the first part of Faniaca's tale is nominally set – Spain and Portugal formed a single political unit, the 'Iberian Union' (Port: União Ibérica), under three successive kings of the House of Austria.

p. 89 *Straights*: i.e. Straits (of Gibraltar).

p. 90 *I saw her sitting at Table*: The story of Faniaca, the sea-captain, his wife, and her lover owes much to international folktale motifs. So, the episode of the adulterous wife very closely resembles a group of folktales – a trickster surprises an adulteress and her lover – found in many cultures, ages, and languages, classified under the Aarne/Thompson system as Type 1358; see Stith Thompson, *The Types of the Folktale: A Classification and Bibliography* (Helsinki: Suomalainen Tiedeakatemia, Academia Scientiarum Fennica, 1964), p. 403. Variants of this tale type include accounts of how the food intended for the lover goes to the husband, how the husband attempts to carry off the box containing his wife's lover and how the unfortunate paramour is taken for the devil. The story of Faniaca also contains variations on a number of motifs found in folktales throughout the world, including K1549.8 – woman prepares food for paramour; and K1574.2 – trickster discovers wife's paramour, hides him, and is rewarded by husband; see Stith Thompson, *Motif-index of folk-literature: classification of narrative elements in folktales, ballads, myths, fables, mediaeval romances, exempla, fabliaux, jest-book and local legends*, 6 vols (Bloomington: Indiana University Press, 1955–8), 4, pp 406, 407, 410.

p. 90 *hungry Spain*: A characterization found elsewhere in seventeenth-century writing; see James Howell, *A German Diet, or the Balance of Europe* (London, 1653): 'Both Italy and hungry Spain …', p. 18.

p. 90 *two-handed*: Big, bulky, strapping (*OED*, a. 3).

p. 91 *Sea Bisket*: Sea biscuit was a staple food on board seventeenth-century vessels.

p. 91 *St. Jago*: i.e St. James the Elder (Sp: Santiago), the patron saint of Spain.

p. 91 *Witch* The reputation of non-Inca American Indian women as witches is discussed by Garcilaso in *Royal Commentaries*, I, vi, 'Of the different ways of Marriages, and diversity of Languages amongst them. And of the Poisons and Witchcrafts that they used', which includes the passage: 'Witchcraft was more commonly used by the Women, than by the Men, who, to gain a reputation to themselves of Wisedom [*sic*], of Prophecies and Predictions of things to come, like *Pythonesses,* or *Sibyls,* treated familiarly with the Devil' (p. 10), and elsewhere; while the Spanish invaders were characteristically dismissive of American Indian claims to be able to foretell the future, especially by raising the Devil, Garcilaso notes several instances of accurate prognostications (see, for instance, Part 2, VII, xx, p. 956).

p. 92 *enter into it himself*: The lover hidden in a chest to avoid detection and mistaken for a devil combines two related, international folkloric motifs, K1555.0.2 (paramour in chest) and K1555.2 (devil in the barrel), under the Aarne/Thompson classification system; see Thompson, *Motif-Index of Folk-literature*, 4, pp 407, 408.

p. 95 *Chyrurgeon*: i.e. surgeon.

p. 95 *Inquisition*: The Spanish Inquisition was an ecclesiastical tribunal, charged with maintaining orthodoxy, established by Ferdinand II of Aragon and his wife Isabella of Castile in 1478 (and not abolished until 1834). Technically, it only had jurisdiction over baptized Catholics (which Faniaca is not, at this stage of the narrative).

p. 95 *Maravedy*: The *maravedí* was a Spanish or Portuguese coin, of gold or silver, and of variable value.

p. 96 *The Siege of a City*: Faniaca's narrative now leaps from the late-sixteenth to the late-seventeenth century. The city is Derry, besieged by the forces of the Dutch Protestant Prince William of Orange between 7 December 1688 and 28 July 1689.

p. 96 *Duckets*: i.e. ducats.

p. 96 *Outlandish Woman*: See above, n. to p. 58.

p. 96 *Chester*: Situated on the River Dee, Chester was the principal port in north-west England, especially important for its traffic with Ireland.

p. 96 *A War in Ireland*: The war began in 1688, developing in intensity after the arrival in Ireland of William's army under Marshal Schomberg (see above, n. to p. 40: 'Prince of S——g') on 13 August 1689.

p. 99 *Capricio*: (It: *capriccio*), capriciousness, a sudden whim.

p. 100 *happiness … the possession of what we Love*: A secularized version of St Augustine's belief that the possession of God or the knowledge of God constitutes happiness; see *De moribus ecclesiae catholicae et de moribus Manichaeorum libri duo* (388) 25.47.

p. 102 *Cormorant*: Voracious or rapacious.

p. 103 *Express*: i.e. express message.

p. 103 *the King had set out of Dublin*: Having arrived in Dublin on 5 July, four days after his victory at the Boyne, William marched south to Waterford (rather than west to Limerick) on 8 or 9 July, and was the guest of James Butler, duke of Ormond, at Kilkenny Castle on 19 July. He does not seem to have been in Clonmel at this time though he passed through the town in the first days of September, after the lifting of the first siege of Limerick.

p. 103 *Billet Doux*: (Fr. 'sweet note'), a love-letter.

p. 104 *Papist*: i.e. a Roman Catholic; usually derogatory.

p. 104 *no free-born Irish-woman*: Although it antedates him, the term 'freeborn' is generally associated with the Leveller, John Lilburne (1615?–1657), who came to be known as 'Freeborn John'. The radical political position implied by the epithet is here doubly unusual for the period in being applied both to a woman and an 'Irish'-woman; *OED* 'Free-born' A. *adj*. 1. cites the present usage.

p. 105 *devoir*: Respect.

p. 105 *Leuidores*: (Fr. *louis d'or*) A French gold coin, first minted in 1640, under Louis XIII, and in widespread circulation in England, where its value would be fixed by Act of Parliament in 1717.

p. 106 *Proteus*: A classical sea-god, able to change his shape.

p. 106 *Be Constant and be Happy*: The phrase echoes Seneca: 'It must be a *Sound Mind* that makes a *Happy Man*; there must be a Constancy in all Conditions', Seneca, *Of a Happy Life*, trans. Roger L'Estrange, in *Of a Happy Life, and wherein it consists'*, in *Seneca's Morals*, II, p. 5, as it does also the title of the second edition of Heliodorus's *Ætheopian History* (1686), whose last five books were translated by the Irish-born and educated Nahum Tate: *The Triumphs of Love and Constancy: A Romance containing the Heroick Amours of Theagenes & Chariclea* (1687).

p. 108 *K—k*: As with the use of *S——g* (see above, n. to p. 40), the name teases the reader to make an identification with Major-General Percy Kirk, commander of the Williamite forces at the Siege of Derry; the question of whether the 'great Officer' would 'prove Constant' might conceivably allude to the fact that Kirk had gained the favour of James II by his brutal suppression of the rebellion of the Duke of Monmouth in 1685, only unexpectedly to desert the king for William of Orange.

p. 108 *Jacobus*: An English gold coin, issued under James I.

p. 108 *cozening*: Deceiving, cheating.

p. 108 *Old Man ... Young one*: The character of the amorous old man – the *senex amans* – in competition with the poor young man for the affections of a young woman is a stock one in Greek and Roman comedy, as is the implied solution of cuckoldry.

p. 109 *silver Groat*: Now synonymous with a small sum, the medieval groat was originally equivalent, in theory, to one-eighth of an ounce of silver.

p. 109 *Jigglets*: Not recorded in *OED*, the word would seem to imply inconstancy.

p. 111 *Absence*: 'Absence makes the heart grow fonder' has classical origins – see Sextus Propertius, *Elegies*, II, xxxiii, l. 43 – but does not seem to have been truly proverbial in the seventeenth century.

p. 111 *We have block'd your Enemies up, won a fort from them, and daily gain more ground*: Many of the details of the siege of Limerick, as of other aspects of the military campaign in Ireland in 1690, can be confirmed by reference to contemporary published accounts. The author of *Vertue Rewarded* seems to have drawn particularly from one of the best known of these: that by George Warter Story; see above, 'Introduction', p. 12; the fort was taken on 20 August 1690.

p. 113 *the Irish-Town*: The Irish and English towns of Limerick – i.e the towns home to the Gaelic, Catholic and English, Protestant peoples, respectively – stood on opposite banks of the River Shannon.

p. 113 *that Limerick would soon be taken*: It had been expected that Limerick would fall to the Williamite forces in 1690 but the difficulties posed by Limerick's natural defences, fierce Jacobite resistance, and the onset of bad weather persuaded the king to call a council of war, which determined to lift the siege until the following year, with the result that the army left Limerick on 30 August 1690.

p. 113 *Sarsfeild*: Patrick Sarsfield (*d.* 1693), first earl of Lucan, an Irish Catholic commander in the Jacobite army, led a daring raid against the Williamite siege train, following two days behind the main forces, on 12 August 1690, at Ballyneety, in county Limerick; see above 'Introduction', p. 26.

p. 114 *the days of Errantry are past*: Although *Vertue Rewarded* contains many elements of the older prose romance, such sentiments as these – though they can be traced back at least as far as Cervantes's *Don Quixote* (1605; 1615) – suggest the author's desire to write a modern 'novel', in contrast to the romances described by William Congreve in his preface to *Incognita*: 'Romances are generally composed of the Constant Loves and invincible Courages of Hero's, Heroins, Kings and Queens, Mortals of the first Rank, and so forth; where lofty Language, miraculous Contingencies and impossible Performances, elevate and surprize the Reader into a giddy Delight'; see William Congreve, 'The Preface to the Reader', *Incognita* (London, 1692), pp viii; viii–ix. That such romance sentiments had not disappeared from late-seventeenth century writing is evident from Jonathan Swift's first published work, written shortly after the Battle of the Boyne, in which Swift imagines William III at that battle as a knight errant:

These are the ways
By which our happy Prince carves out his Bays
Thus he has fix'd His Name
First, in the mighty List of Fame,
And thus He did the Airy Goddess Court,
He sought Her out in Fight,
And like a Bold Romantick Knight
Rescued Her from the Giant's Fort ...

For strait I saw the Field maintain'd,
And what I us'd to laugh at in *Romance*,
And thought too great ev'n for effects of Chance,
The Battel almost by *Great William*'s single Valour gain'd.

('Ode to the King on his Irish Expedition and the Success of his
Arms in General' (1690), ll. 31–8, 61–4)

p. 114 *Apollo's Brain to invent*: In classical mythology, the many-faceted god Apollo is often identified with the sun and, as god of music, has the cithara (or lyre) as one of his many attributes.

p. 115 *The Prince … was gone out of Town*: The Williamite army broke up in mid-September, with units variously dispersed in Waterford, Cashel, and Clonmel, besides Dublin; see Story, *Impartial History* (1691), pp 136–7.

p. 115 *the shrieks of one in distress*: The episode that follows concerns an attack by rapparees, or Irish irregulars. Rapparees operated in various parts of the country between 1689 and 1691 and were especially active around Clonmel. In Story's *Impartial History* (1691), the breaking up of the Williamite army (see preceding note) is immediately followed by the information that 'a Party of Horse were sent after a Company of *Rapparees* that had kill'd some of our Men as they were a forraging' (p. 137). For the continuing activity of rapparees around Clonmel, see James Shirley, *True and Impartial History*, pp 124–8.

p. 116 *Teague's weapon*: Teague is a pejorative term for an Irishman, here one of the 'mere' or 'wild' Irish. Although the term 'rapparee' seems to derive from the Irish *rápaire* (a rapier or short pike), the pitchfork was often associated with rural violence in Ireland.

p. 116 *mittimus*: Among other meanings, mittimus denotes a dismissal; here, by extension, a very final dismissal.

p. 117 *tedious*: Tiring, painful.

p. 117 *Beavor of his Morion*: The visor of his helmet.

p. 117 *Rapparees*: See above, n. to p. 115, 'the shrieks of one in distress'.

p. 120 *Diana*: In Roman mythology, Diana was goddess of the hunt but also associated with the moon and, most relevantly here, was the emblem of chastity.

p. 121 *Ballsom*: i.e. balsam; used for healing wounds and soothing pain.

p. 122 *Gust*: Taste (Fr. *goût;* It. *gusto*).

p. 123 *Potosi*: A town in modern Bolivia, Potosí was founded by the Spanish as a mining settlement in the mid-sixteenth century, and was the source of the bulk of the vast quantity of silver shipped into Europe between the sixteenth and eighteenth centuries.

p. 124 *Banes*: i.e. banns (of marriage).

p. 125 *byassed*: i.e. biased.

p. 128 *Guzman*: Spanish surname, historically with aristocratic connotations.

p. 129 *Hollanders raising Souldiers*: See above, n. to p. 40, 'Forreign Troops'. The chronological compression that characterizes 'The Story of Faniaca' finds its counterpart here in the story of Astolfo; see above n. to 'The Siege of the City', p. 96.

p. 129 *the* English *came over to our side*: William of Orange landed at Torbay on 5 November 1688 OS; although support was slow to materialize, he was able to enter London in December without the anticipated fighting.

p. 129 *Schomberg*: This is the first mention by name of Duke Frederick Herman von (or de) Schomberg, commander of the Williamite army, killed at the Boyne; see also above, n. to p. 40, 'Prince of S——g'.

p. 130 *the Church*: Whether intentionally or not, the nature of Faniaca's conversion from paganism to Christianity is obscure, leaving doubt as to whether she becomes an Anglican Protestant or whether she becomes a member of the Roman Catholic church, like her husband-to-be Astolfo.

p. 131 *the Coyest Lady ... is to be won*: Perhaps inadvertently, the sentiments recall the final stanza of 'As Chloris full of harmless thought', by John Wilmot, earl of Rochester (1647–80):

> Thus she who *Princes* had deny'd,
> With all their *Pomp* and *Train;*
> Was in the lucky *Minute* try'd,
> And yielded to the *Swain*.

Poems on several occasions by the Right Honourable the E. of R—— (Antwerp [i.e. London], 1680), p. 58, 'Song', ll. 21–24.

List of emendations

The present text respects the spelling and punctuation of the first edition of *Vertue Rewarded*, with the exception of the emendations noted below, and the conventions used to denote direct speech (see 'A Note on the Text', p. 31 above). For the introduction of paragraphing, see 'A Note on the Text' also.

p. 56, l. 16up: Mistress's] Mistresses's
p. 64, l. 9up: Yet] yet
p. 75, l. 6: *Amaru*] *Amanu*
p. 78, l. 6: danger,] danger)
p. 79, l. 10up: destruction] destrustion
p. 89, l. 15: she laughing] she (laughing
p. 100, l. 18up: Love has not so] Love has so
p. 103, l. 18: *Billet Doux*] *Billet Deux*
p. 119, l. 11up: would] woold
p. 120, l. 9up: *Marinda*] *Marinda,*
p. 122, l. 14up: *desires*] *deseres*
p. 123, l. 10: Celadon,)] Celadon,
p. 127, l. 6up: *Brothers,* laid] *Brothers* laid
p. 127, l. 5up: another, thence] another thence

Appendix: Marinda and the authorship of *Vertue Rewarded*

Vertue Rewarded; or, The Irish Princess is of uncertain authorship. Given the frequency with which fiction was published anonymously in the seventeenth and eighteenth centuries, this is not especially surprising. What is more remarkable is that there is good reason to believe that the novel was originally written for a specific reader whose plausible identification tantalizingly suggests an intriguing candidate for authorship.

The dedicatory epistle is directly addressed to 'the Incomparable *MARINDA*' (p. 35), with the author declaring that 'in describing the *Marinda* of this Novel, I borrow from you, not only her Name, but some of the chief Beauties I adorn her with' (p. 35). However conventional the complimentary reference to the lady's qualities may be, the insistence that the heroine's name is borrowed from the dedicatee is more unusual. The likelihood that the dedicatee was an actual, historical person is reinforced in the preface that follows, where the author declares: 'I Printed it [*Vertue Rewarded*] for the ease of her whom it was made for' (p. 37). The striking assertion that the heroine's name is 'borrowed' from the dedicatee is significantly reinforced by the otherwise inexplicable gloss: a statement that would appear to suggest that the work derived from an anterior version, as oral narrative or manuscript.

If such preliminary material suggests there might be a real Marinda for whom *Vertue Rewarded* was written, and to whom it is dedicated, an identification of the original reader becomes possible. Despite the use in the novel of names drawn from verse or prose romance – Astolfo is a character in Ludovico Ariosto's *Orlando Furioso* (1532); Celadon, the confidant of the Prince, shares a name with one of the pastoral heroes of d'Urfé's *L'Astrée* (1607–28) – Marinda was not a familiar name in the seventeenth century.[1]

Despite this, a candidate does, in fact, readily present herself, for 'Marinda' was the coterie name adopted by Mary Molesworth, daughter of Robert (later Viscount) Molesworth (1656–1725) and his wife Laetitia. It was Robert Molesworth who, following his daughter's death in 1715, oversaw the publication of a volume of poems by and to his daughter, under the title *Marinda: Poems and Translations upon Several Occasions* (1716).[2] Mary Molesworth's date of birth

---

1 See n. to p. 35, 'Marinda', pp 137–8.
2 *Marinda: Poems and Translations upon Several Occasions* (London, 1716).

is not certain. When Robert Molesworth drew up his Genealogia Antiquæ Familiæ de Molesworth, dated 1688, Mary was recorded as 'filia secunda genita ætat 8 annor. Ao 1688', which would make her 12 or 13 when *Vertue Rewarded* was published.[3] The second daughter of the seventeen children of Robert and Laetitia, daughter of Richard, Lord Coote of Coloony, Mary would marry George Monck of Dublin, who later became member of the Irish parliament for Philipstown, thanks to the patronage of his father-in-law. Little is known of their marriage, though it seems to have ended unhappily.

Apart from the fact of her coterie name, Marinda, what makes Mary Molesworth an intriguing candidate for the dedicatee of *Vertue Rewarded* is her family background in Ireland. Shortly after the publication of *Vertue Rewarded*, Robert Molesworth, a staunch supporter of William III, gained celebrity (or notoriety) for his *Account of Denmark, as it was in the year 1692* (1694), which suggested Lutheran Denmark to be an arbitrary and tyrannical society, attacked the connection between church and state, and offered a defence of liberty that did not go unchallenged in contemporary England, still less in Ireland in the immediate aftermath of the post-Williamite settlement. A well-known figure in contemporary Irish political and literary circles, Molesworth was also in the early 1690s in close epistolary and personal contact with Sir Paul Rycaut, the translator of Garcilaso de la Vega's *Royal Commentaries*, source of all the Peruvian material in *Vertue Rewarded*'s interpolated story of Faniaca.[4]

Born in 1629, Rycaut had had a full and varied career as a diplomat, especially in Turkey, north Africa, and the Levant, and as a writer, notably as author of *The Present State of the Ottoman Empire* (1667).[5] He was knighted in 1685 and, in the following year, appointed Chief Secretary to Ireland, in which role he accompanied the new lord-lieutenant, the Earl of Clarendon, to Dublin. In the autumn of 1686, Rycaut traveled with Clarendon on a tour of the southern part of the country that included a visit to Clonmel, where he lodged with a Mr. Hamerton, while the Viceroy was entertained by a wealthy gentleman named Moore.[6] It was while he was in Ireland that Rycaut wrote part of his translation

---

3   We are grateful to William Molesworth for this transcription of the relevant section of the genealogy (Molesworth Trust, roll on vellum). In *ODNB*, J.M. Ezell tentatively suggests a 1677 date of birth for Mary Molesworth, but does not state her grounds for this; see 'Mary Monck [née Molesworth]', *ODNB*, 38, pp 592–3.

4   See above, 'Introduction', pp 20–4.

5   For the best general account of Rycaut, see Sonia P. Anderson, 'Sir Paul Rycaut (1629–1700)', *ODNB*, 48, pp 439–42; and see also Anderson, *An English Consul in Turkey: Paul Rycaut at Smyrna 1667–1668* (Oxford: Clarendon, 1989).

6   For Rycaut in Ireland, see Patrick Melvin, 'Sir Paul Rycaut's Memoranda and Letters from Ireland 1686–1687', *Analecta Hibernica*, 27 (1972), 123–82, and K.T. Hoppen, *Papers of the Dublin Philosophical Society, 1683–1708* (Dublin: Irish Manuscripts Commission, 1980), p. 189. Rycaut also had family connections with Ireland – his brother was a prominent Dublin lawyer – and he became a member of the privy council, a judge of the Admiralty, and was elected to the council of the Dublin Philosophical Society.

of Garcilaso's *Comentarios reales*. When James II's viceroy, the earl of Tyrconnell, began to implement his process of Catholicization, however, Rycaut and Clarendon were both relieved of their positions, leaving the country in 1687. After a spell in London, Rycaut was appointed by the new monarchs William and Mary to be resident in the Hanse towns of Hamburg, Lübeck, and Bremen. Known to Robert Molesworth in the Ireland of the 1680s, and with friends in common, Rycaut corresponded with him in 1691–2, later entertaining him, and arranging accommodations for his wife and family, in Hamburg, as they made their separate ways back from Denmark, after Molesworth's recall, in July 1692.[7]

Does a possible connection between Rycaut, Robert Molesworth, and Mary Molesworth, 'Marinda', allow for an attempt to identify the author of *Vertue Rewarded*? Certainly, the fact that this author had access to a copy of *Royal Commentaries* while writing suggests him (and we believe the author was male) to have been considerably more than a hack writer. *Royal Commentaries* is a folio of over 1000 pages, hence an expensive book and one not easily accessible outside of a sizeable private library. The range of literary and historical reference and allusion in the novel more generally would support the notion that the author was a gentleman of some education, writing at times with sources to hand (as with *Hudibras*, quoted on the title-page, and some account of the Williamite wars of 1689–91, most likely George Story's *Impartial History*) or from a well-stocked but occasionally fallible memory.[8] From the wealth of Irish reference, it seems likely that the author was Irish or knew Ireland and, given the unusual provincial setting, was acquainted with Clonmel. If the suggested identification of the Marinda of the dedication with Mary Molesworth is correct, then the author must also have been a friend of the Molesworth family. Since a close reading of the dedicatory epistle to *Vertue Rewarded* suggests that the work was originally known in a pre-print form (either as an oral narrative or in manuscript), it is tempting to wonder whether Rycaut himself might not have been the author, the occasion of the work being the visit paid by Laetitia Molesworth with her children, including Mary, to Hamburg en route from Denmark to England in 1692, a few months before the publication of the novel. The supposition of Rycaut's authorship would help account for the otherwise puzzling insistence that the work was printed 'for the ease of her whom it was made for', since by the autumn of 1692 Mary Molesworth was in London. So much, however, is speculation that finds no confirmation – though no contradiction either – from surviving records.[9]

7 The authors are indebted for information on these points to Hugh Mayo, who also generously provided us with his transcripts of correspondence between Rycaut and Molesworth held in the British Library (BL Lansdowne 1153C, BL Lansdowne 1153D, and BL Add. MSS 19514).

8 See above notes to '*The Dutchess of Suffolk*' (p. 138) or '*mighty* Scythian ... *Terror of the World*' (p. 142).

9 If it should ever emerge that Rycaut was the author, one might understand *Vertue Rewarded* as a work that, combining romance with Irish and south American colonial history, seeks simul-

Among a small number of other plausible candidates, one other deserves mention: Robert Molesworth himself. Absent from his family for part of 1692, could he have written *Vertue Rewarded* for his daughter? All other considerations aside, Molesworth was a notably loving father who, years later, would place his dying daughter's concerns above political affairs,[10] and who would see to the publication of her verse, in a volume dedicated to a German princess, Caroline (the future queen of England), in which he compliments the dedicatee with the observation that 'one of the greatest *Rewards of Virtue*, is a *well grounded Praise*'.[11]

At all events, if he is ever to be identified, it would seem to be within the family, social, or political circles in which Robert Molesworth moved in the early 1690s that the author of *Vertue Rewarded* is to be found.

taneously to address two quite different audiences: the young Mary Molesworth and her father Robert Molesworth. It should be noted, however, that Sonia P. Anderson, the greatest contemporary authority on Rycaut, who kindly considered an extended version of this theory, is adamant in her belief that Rycaut himself was *not* the author of *Vertue Rewarded*.

10 See letter of Robert Molesworth to the earl of Sunderland, 11 June 1715: 'I continued out of town during the holydayes with a sick daughter ...' (BL Add. 61639 187).

11 *Marinda*, p. [vi].

Select bibliography

PRIMARY TEXTS

a) Vertue Rewarded

[Anon.]. *Vertue Rewarded; or, The Irish Princess. A New Novel.* London: Richard Bentley, 1693.

[*Vertue Rewarded* appeared, with a separate title-page, and separately paginated, in Volume XII of *Modern Novels*, 12 vols. London: Richard Bentley, 1692–3.]

[Anon.]. *Vertue Rewarded; or, The Irish Princess*, ed. Hubert McDermott. The Princess Grace Library Series 7. Gerrards Cross: Colin Smythe, 1992.

b) Other Sources

El Ynca Garcilaso de la Vega. *Comentarios reales.* Lisbon, 1609.

—. *Historia General del Peru.* Cordoba, 1617.

—. *Royal Commentaries of Peru*, trans. Sir Paul Rycaut. London, 1688.

—. *Royal Commentaries of the Incas, and the General History of Peru*, trans. Harold V. Livermore. 2 vols. Austin: University of Texas Press, 1966.

[Story, George]. *A True and Impartial History of the most material Occurrences in the Kingdom of Ireland during the last two years with the present state of both armies: published to prevent mistakes, and to give the world a prospect of the future success of Their Majesties arms in that nation, written by an eye-witness to the most remarkable passages.* London, 1691.

—. *A Continuation of the Impartial History of the Wars in Ireland from the time that Duke Schomberg landed with an army in that Kingdom, to the 23d of March 1691/2, when Their Majesties Proclamation was published, declaring the war to be ended … together with some remarks upon the present state of that kingdom.* London, 1693.

—. *An Impartial History of the Wars in Ireland, with a continuation thereof in two parts.* London, 1693.

SECONDARY TEXTS

Vertue Rewarded; or, The Irish Princess

McDermott, Hubert. 'Introduction', in *Vertue Rewarded; or, The Irish Princess*, Princess Grace Library: 7 Gerrards Cross: Colin Smythe, 1992. Pp v–xxxix.

Markey, Anne and Ian Campbell Ross. '*Vertue Rewarded; or, The Irish Princess*: Clonmel in a Seventeenth-Century Irish Novel', *Tipperary Historical Journal* (2007), 45–54.

Ross, Ian Campbell and Anne Markey. 'From Clonmel to Peru: Barbarism and Civility in *Vertue Rewarded; or, The Irish Princess*', *Irish University Review*, 38:2 (2008), 179–202.

Ross, Ian Campbell. 'Ottomans, Incas, and Irish Literature: Reading Rycaut', *Eighteenth-Century Ireland*, 22 (2007), 11–27.

Salzman, Paul. '*Vertue Rewarded* and *Pamela*', *N&Q*, New Series 26 (1979), 554–5.

—. *English Prose Fiction 1558–1700*. Oxford and New York: Oxford University Press, 1985.

Seventeenth- and Eighteenth-Century Prose Fiction

Aravamudan, Srinivas. *Tropicopolitans: Colonialism and Agency, 1688–1804*. Durham, NC: Duke University Press, 1999.

Backscheider, Paula R. and Catherine Ingrassia (eds). *A Companion to the Eighteenth-Century English Novel and Culture*. Oxford: Blackwell, 2005.

Carnell, Rachel. *Realism, Partisan Politics and the Rise of the British Novel*. Basingstoke: Palgrave Macmillan, 2006.

Davis, Lennard J. *Factual Fictions: The Origins of the English Novel*. New York: Columbia University Press, 1983.

Doody, Margaret Anne. *The True Story of the Novel*. London: HarperCollins, 1997.

Douglas, Aileen. 'The Novel before 1800', in John Wilson Foster (ed.), *The Cambridge Companion to the Irish Novel*. Cambridge: Cambridge University Press, 2006. Pp 22–38.

Hammond, Brean and Shaun Regan. *Making the Novel: Fiction and Society in Britain, 1660–1789*. Basingstoke: Palgrave, 2006.

Hunter, J. Paul. *Before Novels: the Cultural Contexts of Eighteenth Century English Fiction*. New York: W.W. Norton, 1990.

Keymer, Thomas and Peter Sabor. *Pamela in the Marketplace: Literary Controversy and Print Culture in Eighteenth-Century Britain and Ireland*. Cambridge: Cambridge University Press, 2007.

Kilfeather, Siobhan. 'Sexuality 1685–2001', *Field Day Anthology of Irish Writing, Vols IV and V: Women's Writing and Traditions*, ed. Angela Bourke and others, 5 vols. Cork: Field Day and Cork University Press in association with Field Day, 2002. Vol. 4. Pp 755–824 (766–8).

Loveman, Kate. *Reading Fictions, 1660–1740: Deception in English Literary and Political Culture*. Aldershot: Ashgate, 2008.

MacCarthy, B.G. *The Female Pen: Women Writers and Novelists, 1621–1818*. 1944–7; repr. with an introduction by Janet Todd. Cork: Cork University Press, 1994.

McKeon, Michael. *The Origins of the English Novel, 1600–1740*. 1987; new ed. Baltimore, MD, and London: Johns Hopkins University Press, 2002.

Mayer, Robert. *History and the Early English Novel: Matters of Fact from Bacon to Defoe*. Cambridge: Cambridge University Press, 1997.

Palmeri, Frank. *Satire, History, Novel: Narrative Forms, 1665–1815*. Newark: Delaware University Press, 2003.

Ross, Ian Campbell. 'Fiction to 1800', in Seamus Deane, with Andrew Carpenter and Jonathan Williams (eds), *Field Day Anthology of Irish Writing*, 3 vols. Derry: Field Day, 1991. Vol. 1. Pp 682–759.

—. 'Prose in English 1690–1800: From the Williamite Wars to the Act of Union', in Margaret Kelleher and Philip O'Leary (eds), *The Cambridge History of Irish Literature*, 2 vols. Cambridge: Cambridge University Press, 2006. Vol. 1. Pp 232–81.

Spacks, Patricia Meyers. *Novel Beginnings: Experiments in Eighteenth-Century English Fiction*. New Haven: Yale University Press, 2006.

Warner, William B. *Licensing Entertainment: The Elevation of Novel Reading in Britain, 1684–1750*. Berkeley: University of California Press, 1998.

Bibliography

Loeber, Rolf and Magda Loeber, with Anne Mullin Burnham. *A Guide to Irish Fiction, 1650–1800*. Dublin: Four Courts Press, 2006.